You are cordially invited to...

Honor thy pledge

to the

Miami Confidential Agency

Do you hereby swear to uphold
the law to the best of your ability...

To maintain the level of integrity of this
agency by your compassion for victims,
loyalty to your brothers and sisters and
courage under fire...

To hold all information and identities
in the strictest confidence...

Or die before breaking the code?

KELSEY ROBERTS

AUTOMATIC PROPOSAL

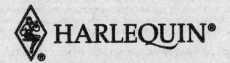

TORONTO • NEW YORK • LONDON
AMSTERDAM • PARIS • SYDNEY • HAMBURG
STOCKHOLM • ATHENS • TOKYO • MILAN • MADRID
PRAGUE • WARSAW • BUDAPEST • AUCKLAND

Acknowledgment
Special thanks and acknowledgment are given
to Kelsey Roberts for her contribution
to the MIAMI CONFIDENTIAL miniseries.

For Bob... Thank you for being my hero
for twenty-five years.

ISBN 0-373-88695-0

AUTOMATIC PROPOSAL

Copyright © 2006 by Harlequin Books S.A.

www.eHarlequin.com

Printed in U.S.A.

ABOUT THE AUTHOR

Kelsey Roberts has penned more than twenty novels, won numerous awards and nominations, and landed on bestseller lists, including *USA TODAY* and the Ingrams Top 50 List. She has been featured in the *New York Times* and the *Washington Post,* and makes frequent appearances on both radio and television. She is considered an expert on why women read and write crime fiction, as well as an excellent authority on plotting and structuring the novel.

She resides in south Florida with her family.

Books by Kelsey Roberts

*The Rose Tattoo
†The Landry Brothers

CAST OF CHARACTERS

Luke Young—Ex-fiancé of Julia Garcia. Owner of a construction firm, he has a difficult past.

Julia Garcia—Former FBI & DEA agent, now works as a seamstress at Weddings Your Way. Close friend of the Botero family—like a sister to Sonya.

Rachel Brennan—Runs Miami Confidential.

Carlos Botero—Multimillionaire who has a stroke while awaiting word on his kidnapped daughter, Sonya.

Sonya Botero—Being held in a jungle by kidnappers.

Juan DeLeon—Laderan politician who is about to marry Sonya, when she's kidnapped.

Maggie DeLeon—Juan's ex-wife in a Laderan institution.

Craig Johnson—The limo driver for the Botero family, who is involved in Sonya's kidnapping.

AJ Taggert—Luke's foster brother, who is in trouble with drug dealers and knows Luke's secrets.

Tommy Anderson—Wants to avenge the murder of his father, Frank.

Betty Anderson—Abused wife of Frank and mother of AJ.

Carmen Lopez—Luke's younger foster sister.

Prologue

Hard to hide a gun beneath a wedding dress, Julia Garcia mused. She had a smile full of nerves as she strapped the weapon into its holster high up on her thigh, then let the bunched fabric drop to the floor. She smoothed the skirt in place. Could you tell?

Critically, she checked her image in the full-length mirror, turning this way and that. Not bad. Fortunately, the heavy cream-colored peau de soie dropped in a straight A line from the natural waist, covering a multitude of sins. And one Walther PPK.

Keeping her attention on the outline of her legs beneath the stiff silk, she walked a few steps back and forth, making sure that not even a hint of the handgun could be seen when she moved.

She made a pretty decent looking bride, she thought, meeting her own eyes in the mirror. Although this wasn't even remotely close to how she'd imagined her wedding day, she still felt a lump of nerves clogging her throat. Not fear nerves, she told herself, more like stage fright nerves. Very appropriate, since this was all an act. Or it was supposed to be. Her heart thudded against her ribs just thinking about him. Which wasn't part of the plan. She wasn't supposed to have feelings for Luke. Not real ones, anyway. Julia dismissed her errant thoughts, chalking them up to stress, pressure, anything but the notion that love at first sight was real.

Luke seemed like a nice enough guy. And he was hot. *Very* hot.

They'd known each other for exactly one week, thanks to her assignment. Although "*known*" was a gross exaggeration. One couldn't really get to know a person in seven short days. Hell, until she'd seen the application for the marriage license, she hadn't even known his middle name.

All that was by design. Her assignment was to learn everything she could about Joe Esterhaus. Luke was collateral damage. Esterhaus was using Luke. *She* was using Luke. The only person who didn't know either of those truths was Luke Young.

Julia guessed he'd be pretty pissed when he found out. Fortunately, she'd be long gone by then. She checked the time again, feeling a knot of impatience in her stomach.

"Where the hell are you guys?" she whispered. The small anteroom smelled faintly of flowers and stale perfume. Julia imagined how many real brides had stood here looking at themselves in the same full-length mirror. She guessed that they'd been filled with anticipation and a touch of fear, but most of all they'd been happy and excited about their bright new futures. Secure in the love of the men they had chosen.

Which was where her illusion shattered. *My future is anything but secure,* she thought, pacing for real now. *Damn it. Come on, you guys, it's hot in here, and this damn dress is starting to make me sweat.* And while her weapon and harness wouldn't show, sweat would, which would reveal her nerves. How many of those imagined brides had walked down the aisle dripping like Niagara Falls?

Stepping over to the door, she opened it a

tiny crack, peering out into the chapel. Esterhaus was in the first row of chairs. On the groom's side. He was a dapper guy in his late forties, with thick, prematurely gray hair. His shoes alone cost more than all four years of her college tuition combined. He might look like a successful entrepreneur, but Julia knew better.

She didn't see Luke. On a personal level, she felt jilted. On a professional level, she was annoyed. This entire con required that the groom show up. "I'm losing it," she muttered softly as she soundlessly closed the door.

Tension. Nerves coiled in every one of her muscles. Where the hell were the other agents? She was going to need backup. They knew that. They should all be sitting in those pews, dressed as wedding guests. Especially with a guy as slippery as Esterhaus.

He was normally surrounded by a half-dozen heavily armed men. But here, in the quintessentially Vegas wedding chapel, he was unguarded.

Perfect.

Just what they wanted.

Everything was in place. Everything but the groom, and the agents who were supposed to swoop in and arrest the son of a bitch seconds before she said "I do."

If they didn't take him now, they'd have no way of linking the drug shipment to him. The DEA needed to put Esterhaus in prison this time. Twice before, they'd been unable to make a case against the narco-trafficker. But this time, thanks to her efforts, they would finally get him off the streets. Until three hours ago, the DEA had no idea how Esterhaus was getting his product into the country. Julia's assignment had been to get the information so that the government could find a way to shut him down.

Esterhaus was far from stupid. Three undercover agents had tried and failed to get close to him in the past. Julia had found a way to succeed where they hadn't. That way's name was Luke Young.

The most solid lead the DEA had was that Esterhaus used his custom home fixture business as a front for his drug trafficking operation. And that he'd been importing cocaine by the ton. But the DEA had rules to follow. Knowing what Esterhaus was doing and proving it were two different things.

So Julia had gotten close to the man by proxy.

Esterhaus had been spending a lot of time cultivating a business relationship with Luke both before and during the home improvement convention that had drawn them all to Vegas this past week.

Esterhaus had created a brilliant system. He hid his drugs in plain sight. According to what Julia had learned, Esterhaus had the drugs pressed, then encased in porcelain bathroom fixtures. All of this was cleverly and expertly done by a series of East Asian manufacturers. Then the components were run through a bunch of offshore shell corporations, making it nearly impossible for the DEA to connect the product directly back to Esterhaus.

Luke Young had unwittingly turned the tables. He had no idea about the drugs, but he was obviously a savvy businessman. His insistence that Esterhaus provide a sample of the custom fixtures before he placed a large order meant the DEA could finally get the proof they needed to put Esterhaus away for a very, very long time.

Agents were at the warehouse now, executing a search warrant. Another team was supposed to be standing by to arrest the drug lord the second they had the evidence in hand. Julia glanced at the clock again, her palms damp with nerves. If the agents didn't show up soon, she'd have to go through with the ceremony. That was part of the arrest plan. Luke seemed like a nice enough guy, but Julia was a career agent, and she had no desire to marry anytime soon. There were a lot of things she'd do for her country, but she wasn't sure marrying a stranger she'd known all of a week, just because her backup couldn't get their act together in time, was one of them.

She whispered an impatient curse, feeling her stomach lurch. Part of her nervousness was normal, and due to the fact that her whole system was on high alert, as it always was before a sting. The other part was a result of trying to decide her next move should the arrest be delayed. Would she get fired if she chose not to say "I do?"

"I get married," she grumbled. If she didn't, she'd surely arouse the suspicions of Esterhaus. If that happened, there was no telling how long it might take for the DEA to get another foothold into the drug cartel.

"Get the lead out, guys," she said under her breath.

But poor Luke. He really seemed like a decent guy. In another time and place, he was the kind of man she'd enjoy getting to know. Once he discovered he was nothing more than a pawn in all of this, he'd probably consign her to the depths of hell.

She drew in a deep breath to calm her pounding pulse. Again she went to the door and opened it, peering out into the small chapel. Esterhaus was still seated in place. Only now, Luke was at the altar.

Seeing him standing there in a dark tux caused her breath to catch in her throat. She hadn't been jilted after all. He epitomized the cliché of tall, dark and handsome.

Julia was five foot six in her stocking feet, yet Luke towered over her by about ten inches. His shoulders were broad, his muscled body tapering down to a trim waist. He was very tanned, a testament to the fact that he was a hands-on kind of construction boss. Julia couldn't see his eyes, but she didn't need to—they were branded on her brain. Deep, rich brown, the color of Cuban coffee; rimmed in dark, inky lashes the same shade as his slightly too long hair.

Julia suffered another pang of guilt. Intellectually, she knew using Luke was the means to a righteous end. Emotionally, and she blamed this on the wedding dress, she didn't want Luke to get hurt. It wasn't like they'd professed their undying love for one another, right? This was just a job.

She adjusted the gown, tugging the strapless silk bodice to a more modest position. She smiled wryly. Stupid time for her Catholic school upbringing to rear its ugly head. Maybe it wasn't her nun-induced sense of propriety. Maybe it was just that she didn't want her fellow agents bursting through the door and getting an eyeful of her breasts.

If she had an hour and a sewing machine, she could alter the dress. Some people knitted to relax. She sewed, and she was damn good. Maybe an inch of lace across the bodice; she could take it from the hem, no problem.

What was she thinking about sewing for? Where the hell were those agents? She rolled her eyes at the idiotic turn of her thoughts.

She jumped when someone rapped gently on the door.

"We're ready!" she heard the wedding assistant call.

Julia sucked in a breath and let it out slowly. Depending on nothing more than hope that the agents found what they needed *fast*—like, before she turned into Julia Young—she grabbed up the pale pink roses tied with a satin ribbon, and reached for the door.

"Here Comes the Bride" was piped in through the speakers embedded in the ceiling as Julia began a slow walk down the aisle with her gun strapped to her thigh. She was ready.

She looked nervous. Terrified, actually. Luke shifted his weight from foot to foot and battled the strong urge to yank at the tight collar cinched around his throat.

Even looking as if she was walking into the path of an oncoming train, Julia was the most beautiful woman he'd ever seen. She was dark and exotic, inspiring all sorts of fantasies he felt certain were inappropriate in a church. Well, church was a stretch. The Chapel of Love was more like a matrimonial weigh station.

What in the hell am I doing? Luke wondered for the umpteenth time that day.

This wasn't like him. He didn't do things on a whim. He was not an impulsive kind of guy. Every decision, no matter how small, was approached with care and deliberation. A lesson well-learned by the age of seventeen.

But life's lessons and pretty much every

other rational thought zinged right out of his brain within seconds of laying eyes on his approaching bride.

She was close enough now for him to catch the scent of her perfume. Something unexpectedly floral. Sunlight glinted off the sheen of her dress. Well, it wasn't a dress so much as it was a whisper of fabric outlining her shapely top half and hiding the just as shapely lower half in a mile of cream-colored material.

That was just one of the things he admired about his future wife. She had a woman's body. Full and sexy as hell. Just seeing a hint of her deep cleavage sent his mind back into the gutter. He wasn't alone, either. Luke noticed that his about-to-be new supplier had his eyes glued on Julia.

Luke suffered a surprising surge of jealousy. *I've known this woman a week and I'm feeling proprietorial?* his brain challenged. Either he was crazy in love or just plain crazy. His eyes met Julia's as she approached and his heart skipped a beat, as it always did when he saw her.

She didn't look nervous or unsure now. She looked like a serene and beautiful bride approaching the man she intended to spend the rest of her life with. Their love would grow, Luke was sure.

Keeping his eyes on her, he prodded his emotions. Was he sure about this? It was a hell of a commitment based on very little.

He needed to make up his mind now.

He considered turning on his heel and running, but then he looked into those incredible eyes of hers. They were a pale gray, the same shade as a storm cloud just beginning to gather strength.

The deep, rich caramel tinge to her skin set off the lightness of her eyes. She'd left her long, curly black hair loose, allowing it to fall freely over her bared shoulders.

Luke could imagine himself brushing aside the silken strands and kissing his way along her collarbone to the pulse point at her throat, then higher still until he was treated to the taste of her full, glossed lips.

He practically groaned aloud from the effect of his vivid mental image.

Julia took her place beside Luke, struggling to keep her smile in place. Where the hell was the arrest squad?

The music stopped and the Internet-ordained minister smiled up at her. "Let us begin."

Julia swallowed and nodded, wondering if

some strange quirk of fate was going to bind her to a stranger. Her hands were shaking as they gripped the bouquet.

Fixing her eyes on the knot of Luke's tie, she struggled to keep from glancing over her shoulder to check on the focus of the sting.

"Do you, Luke, take this woman to be your lawfully wedded wife?"

"I do."

Impressive. Luke hadn't hesitated at all. Julia wasn't sure she could still speak English as her turn approached.

"Julia, do you take this man to be your lawfully wedded husband?"

"I—" The door at the back of the chapel burst open, letting in a stream of sunlight and a dozen windbreaker-clad agents. Relief and regret vied as Julia turned to the door, then back to face Luke. "Apparently," she said apologetically, "I don't."

Chapter One

Miami, 2006

"You're too close to this one, Julia."

Rachel Brennan didn't even bother to look up as she sat behind the large glass-and-chrome desk. Because she was the head of Miami Confidential, her word should have been final.

Julia didn't see it that way. She was so angry and worried and frustrated she wasn't seeing much of anything. But she knew her only hope of changing Rachel's mind lay in convincing her boss that she was capable of working the Botero case without letting her personal feelings interfere. They'd been through this more than once since the kidnapping of Sonya Botero a couple of weeks ago. Rachel kept insisting Julia help out, but from behind the scenes. Julia wanted a more active role and refused to settle for anything less.

The three chunky, brightly colored, acrylic bracelets on Julia's right wrist clanked loudly as she braced her fingertips against the edge of the desk.

Rachel grudgingly lifted her clear blue eyes. "Was there a particular letter in the word *no* you didn't understand?"

Julia didn't so much as blink at the caution in the other woman's tone. "I'm not a liability, I'm an asset. I've known the Botero family since I was a kid. C'mon, Rachel, I lived with Sonya my last year of high school. Mr. Botero trusts me. I'm like a daughter to him."

"Which is why you need to take a seat. Look…" Rachel paused to put her pen down next to a neat stack of folders. "Getting Sonya Botero back from her kidnappers is our top priority. I won't have the job compromised because you've got a personal connection to the victim and her family."

"How will I compromise the assignment?" Julia argued. "If anything, my affection for the Boteros only makes me more determined to find Sonya and bring her home safely."

Rachel leaned back in the deep red, glove-leather executive chair, stroking the tip of one perfectly manicured fingernail across her chin. The woman looked more like a pageant contestant than the head of a group of highly trained Confidential agents. Her ebony hair was piled loosely on top of her head, secured with a lapis clip that matched the color of her eyes. In spite of the legendary south Florida heat and humidity, Rachel's makeup was fashion-model perfect. But looks were deceiving. Julia knew that Rachel was a legend in the business.

"You're one of the best agents I've ever worked with, Julia," Rachel said. "You've got a great future ahead of you. I don't want to see that derailed because you let your personal feelings prevent you from—"

"They won't," Julia interrupted. "Have I ever been anything but completely professional?"

"No," her boss answered with complete candor.

"Then trust me, Rachel. Trust that I'm a team player who is capable of keeping my focus."

"You're a *frustrated* team player," Rachel replied pointedly.

Julia refused to let her shoulders slump. *So we're going to beat this dead horse again.* "I came to Miami Confidential because I wanted more responsibility and more autonomy than I had with the DEA."

"Which you will get," Rachel repeated.

Julia bit back the urge to ask how many more gowns she'd have to sew or tuxedos she'd have to alter before that became a reality. She wanted to be a full-time agent, not a seamstress. "And I appreciate your faith in me. I'm just asking you to extend that faith to include me in the Botero case. I swear you won't be disappointed, Rachel. Have I ever let you down? Let the team down? Even once? I'm practically a member of the Botero family. You don't have anyone else as close to them. I'm an asset," she repeated, to make her point.

Reluctantly, Rachel shook her head. "I don't think this is a good idea, Julia."

Julia held both her breath and her tongue; it sounded as if her boss was waffling.

"But against my better judgment I'm finally going to say yes, because you're right about being an asset. You're not going to be the primary," she told her flatly. "But your connection to the Botero family *might* be useful. Just don't let any personal feelings for the victim blind you to what has to be done. I expect you to do your job, and remain professional and focused at all times."

"I will." Julia's heart rate increased. "Thank you," she said, exhaling the breath she'd been holding as she began backing out of the well-camouflaged offices. "You won't regret this."

Rachel tossed out a stern look. "See that I don't."

Nodding, Julia felt behind the bookcase and found the keypad that opened the secret door. Half afraid that Rachel would change her mind, she decided a hasty exit was the best option.

Using the back stairway, she entered the public area of Weddings Your Way. The scent of coffee mingled with the fragrance of freshly cut flowers as she moved across the polished tile floor toward her office.

No one would ever have guessed that the upscale Miami business was actually a front for one of the most specialized agencies in the country. Confidential agents worked out of branch offices all over the United States. Because of her sewing skills, Julia had been assigned to Weddings Your Way.

The obvious benefit was the location. Miami was her home, and after four years of moving all over the place at the whim of the DEA, she was all too ready to return to the warm, tropical, familiar surroundings of her childhood.

Julia's office was a large space that occupied the northwest corner of the second story of the converted Spanish-style home on the shore of Biscayne Bay. A wide partition separated her desk from the actual sewing area.

Sidestepping two bolts of fabric leaning against the wall, she slipped behind her cluttered desk, sat down and began flipping through her Rolodex.

Though she and Sonya had been as close as sisters, Julia's work as an undercover agent had created a distance between them. She felt a pang of guilt now, regretting every opportunity lost to fix the breach in their relationship, as she hunted for Sonya's exact address and the code that would get her past the building's security and into Sonya's condo.

Regret was tempered by the resurgence of anger as she remembered the way Sonya had been snatched, right out front of Weddings Your Way. The Botero family was very, very rich. Uncle Carlos had his fingers in all sorts of pies, so the possibilities of who was behind the kidnapping of his only daughter were pretty much endless. Added to that, Sonya's fiancé, Juan DeLeon, was a prominent and controversial politician in Ladera. Politics and kidnapping—particularly in struggling, corrupt South American countries—went hand in hand.

A preliminary investigation on the Laderan angle was already being investigated by Isabelle and Rafe, two other Confidential agents. So Julia decided she should focus, at least for now, on the home front.

Scribbling down the address, she glanced over and saw the message light blinking. She thought about ignoring it, but knew better. No one was more persistent and demanding than a frazzled bride, and the last thing she needed was to compromise the Weddings Your Way front by allowing a bride to suffer a psychotic break.

The first two messages were from suppliers; the beads she'd ordered were finally on their way via overnight express, and the company in Ireland would ship the lace she'd been waiting on by the end of the week.

The last call was from Carmen Lopez, whose wedding was the following week. Julia smiled when she heard her say, "I hate to be a bother, but…" Carmen was a sweet woman who apologized with every other breath.

"My brother will be in your area this afternoon. I told him it would be okay if he stopped in for his fitting around three. If that's a problem, you can call his cell phone." Julia jotted the telephone number on her calendar. "Thank you and I'm sorry to do this on such short notice."

Maybe something had been overlooked at Sonya's place. Checking her watch, Julia decided she had just enough time to go over to the condo, do a second search and be back to meet Carmen's brother for his fitting.

Grabbing up her bulky leather satchel, she dashed out of the building. In no time, she was behind the wheel of her Jeep, the wind blowing through her hair as she crossed the Rickenbacker Causeway and headed toward the oceanfront high-rise Uncle Carlos had given Sonya as a graduation present.

Carlos Botero was a generous man when it came to his daughter. Those qualities had extended to Julia, as well. Thanks to him, when her own father died, the Botero family had given her a home, paid her tuition at St. Francis de Salles High and then sent her to

University of Miami. Had it not been for the kindness of Uncle Carlos, Julia was fairly sure she'd be working in a factory for minimum wage, sewing decorations on straw bags for the throngs of tourists roaming the streets of Little Havana.

Images of Sonya's kidnapping flashed in her brain as she navigated the perfectly groomed street that ran parallel to the Atlantic Ocean. The air was heavy, building toward the inevitable midafternoon thunderstorm. The scent of freshly mowed grass filled her nostrils as she made a left into the secured entrance of the condominium. She would find Sonya, and somehow pay back a little of that kindness.

Pulling the scrap of paper from her purse, she pressed the four-digit code and listened as the metal gates creaked open in a wide, sweeping arc. Julia pulled into the first-floor garage and shoved her sunglasses up on her head, allowing her eyes to adjust to the shadowy interior.

Sonya's cherry-red Porsche was parked in the spot where her unit number was stenciled on the wall. Julia pulled into one of the guest spots and cut the engine.

The heat was oppressive in spite of large

fans mounted near the elevators. The garage smelled dank, and occasional patches of beach sand crunched beneath her shoes as she walked to the entrance.

Stepping into the elevator was like stepping into the past, and it had nothing to do with Sonya. It was the smell. The faint scent of men's cologne that brought a vivid and immediate image to mind.

Luke Young. The scent was woods and citrus, and a single whiff was all it took for Julia to flash back to when she'd last been in his embrace. Shivering, she rubbed her bared arms. She liked to think that the only reason Luke continued to haunt her after all this time was because of the way things had ended six years ago. Or rather, *not* ended.

After the arrest of Esterhaus in the middle of what should have been their wedding, she'd been a total wimp. And a rude one at that. She'd never returned any of his calls. It wasn't as if she could tell him the truth. The DEA had strictly forbidden her from revealing her role in the sting. Not even to Luke. As far as he knew, she'd just vanished. A jittery almost-bride who had come to her senses. Why did she still care what he might think of her?

A ding sounded, jarring her back to reality as the elevator doors slid open, revealing a beautifully decorated hallway. Sonya's condo, if she remembered correctly, was at the far end of the corridor. She pulled a small zippered pouch from her purse as she approached. By the time she was at the door, she had two small jimmies at the ready.

It took just under seven seconds for Julia to pick the dead bolt, and about half that time for her to dispatch the bottom lock and turn the knob. Ironically, her ability to pick locks was a skill learned not during her years with the DEA or even as part of the rigorous training for Confidential. Rather, she'd mastered this particular ability as a young child. Much to the chagrin of her father.

Julia was only three years old when her family had climbed into makeshift rafts in the dead of night to escape from Cuba to the United States. Like many refugees, freedom had come at a high price. Her mother and older brother had drowned during the crossing, leaving Julia and her dad to build new lives in America alone. As a single father, Ricardo had taken Julia with him to work when she wasn't in school. While he was busy landscaping the lovely lawns of the Miami mansions, Julia developed a fascination for the large homes. By the age of ten she didn't let something like a locked door prevent her from satisfying her curiosity. She never took anything, she just looked, amazed at how other people lived.

"I was damn lucky I wasn't arrested for trespassing," she mused softly.

Once inside Sonya's condo, she was still smiling at the childhood memory, and her smile broadened at the familiarity of the room she hadn't visited often enough over the years. Sonya's home was an extension of her personality. It was bright and cheery and full of color. It also smelled of metallic fingerprint dust left by the crime scene unit going over the place. The maid had been through as well. A good thing since Sonya would have freaked if she ever saw what a search team could do to the place.

"Where to start?" Julia muttered as she dropped her bag onto an upholstered, modern purple chair that looked more like a sculpture than a piece of furniture. Though Sonya had been gone a couple of weeks, the smell of sunscreen lingered in the room. Sonya was a stickler for protecting herself from the harsh UV rays.

Julia could easily imagine her friend on that last morning, rushing around as she prepared to go to Weddings Your Way to finalize some of the details for her wedding to Juan.

Julia frowned as she gazed around the room. "Your fanatical neatness isn't helping me, Sonya."

There wasn't so much as cushion out of place as she walked from the living room through the dining room, then into the kitchen.

The long, narrow room was equipped with top-of-the-line appliances in polished stainless steel. The cabinets were all glass-fronted, with the frames glazed white. The starkness was a perfect backdrop for Sonya's colorful accessories. Julia was drawn to one item in particular, a ceramic soap dish perched at the edge of the sink. It was an amateurish creation, uneven and decorated with badly painted stripes, now used to cradle a sponge.

Lifting it, Julia ran her finger along the chipped edge before securing the sponge and flipping the whole thing over. There, etched into the back of the now-hardened clay, was "las amigas mejor"—best friends. Julia had ruined her nail file scratching the inscription before the dish was fired in the kiln as part of the required tenth grade art class. Sister Mary Intolerance had snagged the nail file and classified it as a dangerous weapon, and Julia had ended up in detention for a week. The punishment had been worth the crime.

"Why would you keep this?" Julia mused, wondering what the good sister would think of the gun in her purse or the backup weapon in the glove box of her car. Made the nail file seem pretty darn tame.

Putting the sponge holder back in its place, she began opening drawers and cabinets. Not much of interest. At the far end of the polished stone countertop, she noticed a light blinking on the telephone's base unit.

Lifting the receiver, she heard a series of rapid beeps, indicating waiting voice mail. She made a mental note to have someone make arrangements with the phone company to dump the messages when she got back to her office.

Finding nothing to inspire any immediate concern, she worked her way back to the master bedroom. Pushing through the double doors, she found herself embraced by a sea of turquoise, accented by splashes of deep coral. Sonya's two favorite colors.

The room was dominated by a huge bed draped in silk. Matching tables bracketed the headboard, both sporting framed photographs of Sonya and Juan.

Julia rubbed her forehead, feeling her insides knot. *Please let her be okay. Please.*

Nothing in the massive closet had been disturbed. Likewise, the dressers were neat and organized. A small bookcase in the space that separated the bedroom from the spa-caliber bath gave her pause.

Julia found a tattered copy of *The Secret Garden.* Tipping it free from the shelf, she opened the book and grinned. "Thank you, Sonya. Remind me never to mock your predictability again." As always, the pages were hollowed out, creating a small, snug home for Sonya's diary.

Prying the smaller book free, Julia watched as a small scrap of paper fluttered soundlessly to the floor. The handwriting was familiar, as were some of the numbers on the paper. She just couldn't place them.

A combination, maybe? There was bound to be a safe in the condo, behind one of the avant-garde paintings, or perhaps hidden in the floor.

Julia began checking the obvious places.

Her hip bumped the nightstand when she searched behind the silk drape, knocking the telephone over. The cordless handset skittered across the floor.

Grabbing up the phone, Julia was suddenly inspired as she remembered where she'd seen the numbers before. Craig Johnson, Sonya's chauffeur, had been hurt during the commission of the kidnapping. In his wallet, they'd found a business card with nine numbers on the back. To date, the MC team had been unable to make neither heads nor tails of them.

Retrieving the slip of paper, she read the numbers again. The last nine were identical to the ones they'd found on the chauffeur. A theory crystallized in her brain. She'd been thinking the numbers were related to a bank account, but what if Craig had jotted down a phone number? Or at least *part* of one? "Add an international code," she said aloud. "Country, city…*maybe?*"

Testing her hypothesis, she pressed buttons, listening to a staticky series of clicks before a man answered. His voice was gravelly as he greeted her in Spanish.

Mentally, she translated the conversation. "Yes, sir. I'm calling from the United States. To whom am I speaking?"

"Ramon," he said. The single word came out stern and guarded.

The name didn't ring any bells. Julia asked, "How is the weather in Ladera today, Ramon?"

"Weather? Fine. Why? Who is this? What do you want?"

She had to think fast. "This is Julia and I'm with the Laderan-American Friendship League." She rolled her eyes at her own lame explanation. "I got your number from the Boteros. They suggested—"

"I don't know any Sonya Botero."

"Really?" *Then how did you know which Botero I was referencing, moron?* "Because they said you might have some ideas about charities in your village that could benefit from our fund-raising efforts. We've collected close to ten thousand dollars and I—"

"I am a simple farmer. I have no charities." The line went dead.

She considered calling back, but figured that would be a futile effort. No, she'd wait until she got back to the office and have Ethan Whitehawk, another Miami Confidential agent, check into it. He was already scheduled to go to Ladera, so it would be no problem for him to scope out whoever this Ramon was.

She hesitated before replacing the phone

on its cradle. There was something weird about the phone call. Weirder than just Ramon-the-farmer supposedly pulling Sonya's first name out of thin air. Maybe it was nothing. Maybe Ramon was a tabloid reader and he'd heard of Sonya because she was a rich American about to marry a Laderan politician. But that didn't explain the odd clicks on the line.

Julia made another mental note. Check the line for a trap. Maybe someone had put a tap or a listening device on it.

Glancing at her watch, she knew she had to leave or she'd be late for the three o'clock fitting. Raking her fingers through her hair, she silently cursed the annoyance of having to juggle two personas. She'd gone through everything in the condo with a fine-tooth comb, but she'd like to stay longer and do it again. And again. Until she found some small crumb of a lead. Unfortunately, she had to get back to the bridal boutique *now*.

The sky had turned threatening by the time she drove away from the condo, this time with the rag top up. In the distance, jagged spikes of lightning flashed down into the churning ocean. Soon the storm would blow ashore. She floored the gas pedal, hoping to make it back to Weddings Your Way before the downpour.

She was a few blocks south, on A1A, when the first large drops began to splat on the windshield. The wind picked up as she pulled into the driveway. The fresh scent of rain-washed air was lost on Julia as soon as she saw the big SUV blocking her way into the garage. *What inconsiderate jerk did that?*

Using her bag as an umbrella, she dashed from the Jeep just as the raindrops turned into a solid wall of water. Taking the front steps two at a time, she reached the covered porch ten seconds too late. Her purse was a lump of soggy leather. The dye from her sandals was already turning her feet an interesting shade of fuchsia. With the exception of a small part of her scalp at the crown of her head, she was drenched.

Droplets of water blurred her vision as she shoved hair off her forehead, then flapped the hem of her gauzy skirt like a dog shaking water from its fur.

A loud clap of thunder vibrated through her whole body. Reaching for the knob, Julia glanced down to assess the damage. The layered pink-and-white tank tops she'd selected that morning were soaked and clinging. Her skirt was practically transparent. It was bad. But not nearly as bad as looking up and seeing those chocolate-colored eyes narrowed in her direction.

Julia's feet felt as if they'd been staple-gunned in place. That was nothing compared to her clenched stomach. The sudden stab of pain was just as real and palpable as if she'd been sucker punched.

He smiled then. A tight, distant expression. "Well, Julia. We meet again."

"Wh-what are you doing here?"

"I'm here for a fitting."

She winced. "You're the brother?" Then her mind replayed a fast-forward version of their conversations from six years earlier. "Wait. You *can't* be the brother. You told me you were an only child."

"And you told me you'd marry me."

Chapter Two

Even drenched, Julia Garcia had the ability to still the breath in Luke's chest. *Why did I mention the wedding?*

She was even more stunning than he remembered. Damp, dark curls framed the perfect oval of her face. As always, he was transfixed by her eyes—big, expressive and a pale, sultry shade of gray that were as hypnotic as a swirl of smoke.

She must hate him. Big time. Given what had happened on their aborted wedding day six years ago, it was no wonder she'd never returned his calls and was now staring at him as though he were something the cat had coughed up. *He* was the one who'd gotten her involved—granted, unintentionally—with a major drug dealer.

Summoning all of his courage, Luke willed his taut muscles to relax. No sense in making this any harder than it already was. He glanced around, realizing that all eyes were trained in their direction. Great. He'd been in her presence less than a minute and already he'd managed to screw it up.

Again.

"Let me give this another shot. Hi, Julia, good to see you again."

She peered up at him warily. "Y-you, too."

"I'm here to be fitted for a tux for Carmen's wedding."

He watched as Julia grabbed a towel off a hook hidden discreetly behind a curtain, and began drying her arms and legs. He swallowed, trying not to groan as he watched the hem of her skirt rise, revealing a good amount of toned, shapely thigh. He began lifting his gaze, which didn't help. She was wearing those clinging T-shirts, the kind with the thin straps. Because the fabric was cotton and wet, very little was left to his imagination. And Luke had an excellent imagination. He'd been thinking about Julia, and what her top was exposing, for half a dozen years. His pump was already primed. He could easily make out the outline of her tiny waist as well as the full swell of her breasts.

This was not going well. Carmen was

right, much to his chagrin. The Weddings Your Way seamstress was Julia Garcia. *His* Julia. His plan had been to waltz into the shop as the poster child for the fully evolved guy. He'd break the ice by making a joke, then apologize for the whole Vegas thing. Let her take his measurements and be on his way. No harm, no foul. That had been the plan. Too bad it wasn't working real well. Still, he'd felt like a jackass for allowing himself to get involved with Esterhaus, a guy he hadn't fully trusted. He'd let a lucrative business deal override his hard-won common sense.

Now Julia watched him with the carefully blank expression one gave a stranger. An unwelcome stranger at that. She smacked her sodden purse into his midsection. "Hold this while I dry off the worst of it."

Luke obediently held her purse, wishing he was the towel she was stroking across her damp, tawny skin. Once she was no longer dripping, Julia slipped off her shoes, grabbed her purse and padded barefoot toward an elaborate marble staircase anchoring the center of the first floor. "My workroom is upstairs. Come on."

Here, boy. She was treating him like the

dog he was, he thought as he followed her. Nodding to the rest of the staff was considerably better than turning his attention to Julia's butt as she climbed the stairs ahead of him.

Apparently fully evolved wasn't working at all.

Nope, by the time Julia had reached the third step, he was pretty much a walking heap of needy testosterone. Not much had changed in the six years since he'd gotten them both tangled in the drug-trafficking Esterhaus mess.

He tried not to notice the gentle sway of her hips. Tried to ignore the faint scent of her tuberose perfume lingering in the air between them. Tried, but failed.

Miserably.

"Nice place," he commented. Croaked, actually, making him really glad that her back was to him. As glad as he could be given that his eyes were now fixed on the tiny tattoo just above her left shoulder blade. He'd lived in Miami long enough to recognize the Cuban flag on sight.

"It is," she agreed as she neared the top of the stairs. "My office is back this way."

Luke realized the second floor was neatly

sectioned into all things wedding. Thanks to Carmen, he was becoming an expert on the subject. She wasn't just getting married, she was having an *event*. He was happy for her and all, but man, it took about the same amount of planning as a shuttle launch. He couldn't believe he and Julia had pulled off their almost wedding in less than a week, drug dealers not withstanding. Their wedding would have been efficient, expedient and just as binding as the one his crazy sister was planning. Hell of a lot cheaper, too.

Passing through the area devoted to invitations and calligraphy, they reached an etched glass door with the word *private* stenciled in gold.

Leaving the door ajar, Julia rounded a cluttered desk and sat down to face him—moving rather stiffly, Luke decided. He took one of the two chairs opposite hers, gripping the armrests as he leaned back against the cushion.

Almost every inch of wall space was utilized by fabric samples, bits of ribbon and lace and various drawings. Most were affixed with push pins. Beneath the tacked items, he spied some photographs. "Your work?" he asked, pointing to a glossy magazine cover in a Lucite frame.

She nodded. "Yes." Her chair swiveled as

she opened one drawer of the credenza behind her desk to retrieve a thick file folder. "Carmen Lopez and Dalton Mitchell, right?"

"Dalton Mitchell *the third,*" Luke remarked wryly. "I'm told the numeral is a big deal in the Mitchell family."

He watched as her features softened. Not so much so that he could consider it a smile, but she no longer looked as if her face was set in concrete.

Her head tilted to one side, causing a curly tendril to fall free from the thick mass of damp hair she'd twisted into a knot at the nape of her long, tapered neck. Luke battled the urge to reach across the desk to tuck it behind her ear. Better for both of them if he stuck to business. He shifted in his seat.

"Carmen said something about a wool tux?" He grimaced. "She was kidding, right? That sure will be comfortable on a hot June day."

Pulling a catalog page from inside the folder, Julia slipped it across the desk, then grabbed a pencil from a holder and used the eraser end as a pointer. "It's luxe wool, very lightweight and breathable. I think you'll be pleased."

He met her eyes and smiled sincerely. "The key is for *Carmen* to be pleased. She started planning this day in elementary school."

His heart skipped a few times when Julia rewarded him with a grudging smile. God, but she was beautiful. Perfect white teeth set against smooth, bronzed skin. And that mouth. Full, pouty lips sheened with a slick gloss that made him want to vault over the desk and kiss her senseless.

One of her perfectly arched brows rose questioningly. "Why did you keep your sister a secret?"

He shrugged and sat back, letting out a long breath as he redirected his thoughts. "Technically, I didn't. Carmen and I aren't blood relations. We spent several years together in the same foster home."

"She adores you." Julia stiffened slightly. "I never would have guessed that you were the wonderful brother she raves about all the time. Not in a million years."

Luke frowned. He'd been hoping for some understanding. "I'm not a schmuck, Julia. That whole Vegas thing was—"

She held up one hand. The bracelets on her wrist clanked loudly in the sudden silence. "Let's not go there."

"I'd like to explain."

"No need," she assured him, opening a drawer and pulling out a bright yellow, cloth tape measure that she draped around her shoulders. "It was a long time ago, Luke. Let's just be glad we didn't go through with what would have been a monumental mistake."

It rankled to hear the undiluted certainty in her tone. Not that he didn't agree, he just didn't like hearing it. "I didn't know Esterhaus was a drug dealer." Annoyed, he raked his fingers through his hair. "Something I would have explained at length if you hadn't disappeared."

She blew out a quick, irritated puff of air. "The DEA agents told me all that. Really, Luke, let's not rehash our brief past. So…" She paused and stood up. "If you'll step into the next room, I'll take your measurements and you can be on your way."

He rose and the chair legs scraped loudly against the tiled floor in the process. "I'm trying to apologize, Julia."

"No need," she repeated, though there was still a hint of frost in her voice. "Really."

The instant Luke Young touched her arm, Julia felt a zing directly into the center of her being. Six years had done nothing to stifle her primal and instinctual attraction to this man. And what that was all about, she had no clue.

"Hang on." Luke gave her arm a gentle squeeze. "Hear me out. I really am trying to clear the air."

The air I can't breathe when you're standing so close? she wondered. Slowly, Julia lifted her eyes, looking directly into his. The sincerity she read in his steady gaze whittled away all pretext. Relenting, she offered him a smile. "You're right. There's no reason we can't be…civil."

Cocking his head to one side, Luke studied her, his dark eyes never wavering. "Civil, eh?" he repeated, openly amused. "In this kind of explosive situation? That could mean anything."

She attempted to shrug out of his grasp. It didn't work. "It means," she said mendaciously, "you should let go."

His smile broadened as he began to stroke slow, tantalizing circles against her suddenly flushed skin. How was it possible that this man could make her want to melt into a puddle of need with just the pad of his thumb? Julia's blood sang in her veins at his barely there touch. Warmth radiated from her arm, sending a surge of heat the full length of her spine. He'd always affected her like this, only six years ago she hadn't appreciated how rare that heat was. In fact, she'd never been so instantly turned on since.

Swallowing audibly, she fidgeted in his light grasp, torn between the intelligent choice of jumping out of reach and the very real desire to press herself against him. She was conflicted.

How did he do this? How could Luke walk back into her life and in under five minutes have her respiration up and her knees threatening to buckle? Every one of her nerve endings pulsated as she stood rigidly, feeling his warm breath wash over her upturned face. Lifting her hand, she placed her palm tentatively against his forearm, and felt singed by the electric current passing between them.

His mouth pulled into a lopsided, cocky half smile that was surprisingly heartwrenching and familiar. Looking into his eyes, she knew immediately that he recognized her attraction and a lot of good old-fashioned lust. The spark was still there. But how could it be?

Nonsense, she told herself very firmly. She

was reading more into this chance meeting than actually existed. She wanted to believe that her overly emotional reaction was due to her concern over Sonya's kidnapping.

But she didn't believe that at all. She knew the powerful sensations assailing her from every angle were due to...*Luke*. Tall, gorgeous Luke.

"Still want me to let go?" he asked softly.

So softly that her addled brain nearly didn't register the deep, soothing timbre of his voice. She was, however, keenly aware of the precise nanosecond that his fingers slipped away.

"If you'll follow me this way..." she said curtly, almost stumbling toward the deep aqua, Lily Pulitzer fabric curtain separating her office from her workroom.

She wanted her composure, but just then, she'd have settled for her shoes. Especially when she stubbed her toe on the corner of the stepladder she kept next to the carpeted platform adjacent to the changing room. The metal clanged loudly, echoing off the mirrored walls.

"You seem nervous," Luke remarked.

He was right behind her, so close that she could feel the breezy tickle of his breath against the nape of her neck. She stepped out of range, but it was impossible to not look at him. He was reflected in all the mirrors.

"You don't need to be."

She took a deep, hopefully calming breath and tried to find her center. A pretty daunting task when she turned and found herself standing in the shadow of six feet four inches of absolute male perfection. Luke had a kind of casual masculinity that drew her like a tractor beam. When he looked at her with those sensual brown eyes, she was half tempted to tear her clothes off right then and there and toss him down onto the floor.

"Where do you want me?" he asked.

Suppressing the obvious retort, Julia pointed in the direction of the platform. "Step up there. This won't take but a minute."

"Take all the time you need."

Kneeling down, Julia pulled the tape measure off her shoulders and realized that her hands were shaking. "I forgot the order form," she lied, spinning and fairly racing back to her office.

After brushing past the curtain, she squished the tape measure in one hand while banging the heel of her other hand against her forehead. *Stop. Stop. Stop! He's just a man. Get a grip on yourself.* Julia stopped pounding her head, realizing that a) it hurt and b) it didn't change the fact that she had a job to do. She rolled her eyes as she let out a frustrated sigh. Why did Luke have to walk into her life at the most inopportune times? Why couldn't they have run into each other in a grocery store? Or at a park, or the beach? Something *normal.* At a time when she wouldn't have to push him away. She couldn't keep Luke now for the same reasons she couldn't keep him then. She had to put the job first. Would there ever be a right time for them?

"Not likely," she grumbled. She couldn't remember the last time she'd been at the beach, and since there was nothing but a jar of mustard dying of loneliness in her refrigerator, the whole grocery store thing wasn't looking very good, either.

"Okay," she whispered, needing a personal pep talk. "I can make this calm, professional and quick." Stretching the tape measure taut between her hands, she plastered a smile on her face and went back to her workroom.

Luke noticed the precision with which

each bolt of fabric was stacked against the next. He hadn't known that Julia could sew. Or that she'd be so good at giving other people the happy-ever-after wedding she hadn't gotten. Fact was, he knew less about Julia than he did about those fancy fabrics. All he knew about fabric was that it could be cotton or dirty, so the fancy stuff was pretty much lost on him.

Julia's return was not. His heart thumped in his chest when he turned and caught sight of the smile that didn't quite reach her eyes. He might not know her favorite color, but he knew she felt the same pull he did. Now what could he do about it so that she didn't run again? Cocking his head in the direction of the bolts, he said, "I never knew there were so many variations on white."

"Brides like choices," she stated, giving him a tellingly wide berth as he stepped back up on the carpeted platform.

"Brides like checkbooks," he countered. "I could feed a small third-world country on what this wedding is gonna cost."

She peeked up at him through her lashes as she knelt beside him and fixed the tape measure to an imaginary spot on the floor next to the heel of his boot. "Feed a lot of third-world countries, do you? Stand naturally."

She rose, bringing the tape up to his shoulders and the smell of her perfume close enough to make him dizzy. In the process, her hair brushed against his forearm. It was a whisper of silky softness that very nearly made him groan. The black tendrils were still damp from the rain. He could smell the remnants of a citrusy shampoo. Luke instantly imagined her standing under the strong spray of his shower, naked and—

"Legs apart, please."

He looked up at the ceiling so that his body focused on something other than his sexual fantasies. He practically gnawed through his lower lip as Julia tortured him by running her deft fingers along his inseam. Luke stood stick straight while she measured every inch of his body. Hopefully, she hadn't noticed that he'd been holding his breath.

"You're all done," she announced, reaching for the small acrylic clipboard hanging on the wall. "We can schedule an appointment with Vicki on your way out."

Luke felt…dismissed. "For what?"

"In about a week, I need you to come by and

try on the tux. We can make any last minute adjustments before the wedding next Saturday."

"It's a suit," Luke countered. "Besides, it's Carmen's day, right? No one will care what I'm wearing."

"Carmen will care. The photographer will care. I'll care."

"Really?" he asked, stroking his chin. "Why?"

"Reputation," she answered, tucking the nub of a pencil behind her ear. "Weddings Your Way prides itself on one hundred percent customer satisfaction."

He found himself hurrying down off the platform to follow her back to her office. Julia had that effect on him. Ever since that first night, Luke had felt as if he was running in a circle, trying to catch up.

Unsuccessfully.

Maybe a different tactic. Instead of going to the door, he sat back down in the chair opposite her desk.

Her brows rose. "Is there something else?"

"I'm not one hundred percent satisfied."

Her smile slipped fractionally. "Excuse me?"

"My customer satisfaction is dependent

on…" he paused and glanced at his bulky, utilitarian watch "…five minutes of your time."

"Um…okay." She studied him guardedly as she slipped behind her desk and slowly took her seat. Propping her fingertips together, she met and held his gaze. "What do you need five minutes for?"

Rubbing his palms against his jean-clad thighs, Luke thought rapidly. He had one shot and couldn't blow it. "Well, we can start with Vegas."

Her head shook slightly, just enough for that distracting curl to fall forward and catch in her lashes. "Not necessary, Luke, really, I—"

He unintentionally silenced her when he reached out and brushed the lock of hair from her face. "Necessary for me," he countered, letting his hand fall away even though he wanted very much to trace his finger from her high cheekbone down the length of her throat. "My satisfaction level is slipping. Remember, I *am* the customer."

"Technically, *Carmen* and her *fiancé* are the customers."

"And Carmen loves me," he said with a satisfied sigh. "She'd be really upset if I—"

Julia held up her hand. "I get the point.

So, do you really want to rehash the whole Vegas mess?"

"I want to apologize. Wanted to for years. I really didn't know about Esterhaus's sideline. I never would have done business with him, let alone put you in a position where you could have been hurt."

She nodded, her expression bland and guarded. "I believe you."

"Then why'd you disappear?"

She shrugged and looked away. "Seeing those DEA agents rush inside that chapel, well, I guess it just reminded me that we didn't really know anything about one another." When she glanced back in his direction, her features seemed more relaxed. "C'mon, Luke, you've got to admit that getting married back then would have been a huge disaster."

"I do admit that," he agreed easily. "Upon reflection." He paused when one dark brow arched at his word choice. "What, you don't think a guy can reflect between beers?" he joked. "Anyway, after some thought, I knew that the DEA crashing our wedding was a blessing. We didn't know enough about each other to make a marriage last." *But we could have learned*, he thought.

"All's well that ends well."

"Great fortune cookie sentiment," he teased, determined to go easy. "I'm just curious as to why you refused to take my calls. I felt like an ass, and wanted to apologize to you in person. I'm sorry it ended the way it did."

"Esterhaus going to prison?"

"Forget Esterhaus. I'm talking about us. Why didn't you return my calls, Julia?"

"What was I supposed to say?"

"Oh, 'I accept your apology, Luke' would have been a great start. At least then I wouldn't have felt so guilty about dragging you into that mess."

"You didn't need to feel guilty," she assured him.

"Of course I did. You were a sweet, naive young woman working her tail off at that Vegas restaurant. You deserved better than getting drawn into some big *thing* with a major drug trafficker."

"You're falling on your sword pretty hard, there," Julia ribbed good-naturedly. "Your version of history makes me sound like I fell from a turnip truck onto the Vegas strip. I was young. I like to think I can be sweet. But I don't ever remember being naive."

"You were," Luke insisted. "You were what? All of twenty-four?"

"You aren't exactly ready for a retirement home," she remarked. "It was Vegas, Luke. We had a week of fun and it just got out of hand. No need for long-term therapy as a result."

"Good, then we can start over."

He watched as she froze in mid-exhale. To her credit, Julia recovered quickly. "Start what over?"

Luke wagged his finger in the air between them. "Us. You and me. We can date."

"No, I…I don't think—"

"You said you didn't hold me responsible for Esterhaus."

"I don't."

"You seemed like you were having fun when we were together, so what's the problem?"

She blinked. "We almost got married." God, how often had she thought of that day? Wondered what it would have been like? If he was half the man she remembered and admired in her dreams.

"*Almost* being the operative word there. I like you, Julia."

"You don't know me."

He smiled, hoping to put her at ease.

"Hence the need for dating. See, we date, get to know one another. See what happens." *Discover if the heat between us will fizzle or sizzle.*

"Nothing's going to happen," she insisted as she got to her feet. "Your five minutes will be up by the time we stop by Vicki's desk to make your follow-up appointment." Grabbing his shirtsleeve, she practically dragged him from the room. "Besides, I can't date a client."

"Technically, I'm not the client, remember?" he asked with a satisfied smile. He practically whistled as they walked down the marble steps to the desk, where a pretty redhead adeptly manned multiple telephone lines.

Julia hurriedly penciled him in for the following week, two days shy of the wedding. He liked seeing her flustered. It was the only peek he got into her closely guarded thoughts. "I'll see you next week."

"Not good enough," he responded. Even though he'd kept his voice low, his remark perked the receptionist right up. She practically crawled up on the desk in order to listen in on the conversation.

Julia's eyes darted around the room. Her

jaw clenched behind a stiff smile. "It will have to be good enough, Luke. The matter is closed." She turned, spine regally straight, and took two steps toward the stairs.

"Julia, I can't let you walk away."

She turned, her eyes blazing smoky fire. "Excuse me?"

"You're blocking me."

"What?"

He pointed in the direction of the stone courtyard and the driveway beyond. "Your Jeep, right?"

She nodded.

"You're blocking my SUV."

She looked pretty pissed as she marched over, grabbed her keys from her soggy purse and went out the door. "I should have known you were the inconsiderate person who parked in front of the garage," she muttered as she stomped along the stones.

"I didn't make it rain on you, Julia," he said as he fell into step beside her. "It isn't like there's a No Parking sign, either."

"It's a driveway," she grumbled. "Luke, you need to st— Get down!"

He wasn't sure what surprised him the most, her strength or what precipitated it.

Julia lunged at him, her shoulder catching

him just beneath the rib cage, forcing the breath from his lungs as she toppled him onto the hard ground. His head bounced once against the pavement, sending strobes of bright white specks into his field of vision.

At first he thought the crack he'd heard was the sound of his skull fracturing. Then he pieced the sound together with the acrid smell of gunpowder and realized what had happened. What was still happening.

He rolled, covering Julia's body with his own as three more shots ricocheted off the stucco, showering them with a stinging spray of cement.

Chapter Three

Using a knowledge of basic physics coupled with years of martial arts training, Julia used her legs for leverage and managed to switch places with Luke. With her heart in her throat, and wishing she wasn't lying here protecting a civilian when she should be up and at them, weapon drawn, she cradled his face tightly to her chest. The squeal of tires faded as a vehicle sped away.

Rearing back, she gently ran her hands along his head and scalp. Her fingers came away bloody. "You're hit," she choked out, anger overlaying the guilt that had started diluting her instincts. "Stay still and—"

"Not *shot*, hit." Luke replaced her probing fingers with his own. "I hit my head." He winced, gingerly feeling for the wound. "What about you?" He scanned her face and body for injury.

Other than coworkers and the Boteros—assuming she could think of some way to rationalize a gunshot—Julia had never had anyone give a damn one way or the other if she was plugged full of holes or not. But she'd think about it and analyze the warm fuzzy feeling later. Right now she was responsible for Luke's injury.

Head wounds bled. A lot. She knew that. Didn't mean she liked knowing the blood belonged to *Luke.* She was trained for this. He wasn't. "I'm fine," she told him absently, glancing down the street the way the vehicle had peeled rubber. Gone, of course.

"And fast," he remarked, bringing Julia's attention back to him. His gaze wandered over every inch of her until his jaw relaxed and his frown of concern eased from between his brows. "You flattened me. Then you flipped me like a pancake. You're a lady of many talents. How'd you do that?"

"Self-defense classes," she muttered, then ripped a strip of fabric from her skirt and pressed it against his injury. There was a good amount of blood, but that was pretty standard with a head wound. Shallow but showy. By the time she and Luke untangled themselves from each other, Rafe Montoya and Jeff Walsh were racing from Weddings Your Way, guns poised.

It was going to be hard to lie her way out of this one. And not just for the obvious reasons. This was getting really complicated, really fast.

"Everyone okay?" Montoya asked as he held out a large hand to help her up.

Luke ignored Walsh's offered hand as he rose to his feet. "Let's go back inside. I'd like to make sure that you're really not hurt. That was a damn hard fall you took."

Julia gave him a small smile. "I'm fine. I have a hard head."

Who'd been in the car? Who was the shooter? Obviously someone who wanted her dead. Did it have anything to do with her trip to Sonya's? Geez. She needed to make a list of her enemies. That would take awhile.

"Not as hard as the sidewalk," Luke said firmly, holding her arm as if he thought she'd faint at any second. Faint or *run*, Julia mused, feeling another spurt of guilt.

She'd been stunned speechless when Luke had apologized for the wedding fiasco six years ago. Stunned but not about to tell him the real reason she'd run, nor why she'd refused to answer his calls. She would absolve him of his guilt, and keep her own guilt close to her chest. Better for both of them. Especially since things weren't going to change.

His fingers felt warm on her skin. She'd like nothing more right now than to have a moment to lean into him and absorb his solid warmth. His strength. But that wasn't who she was.

Luke lifted her chin with his hand. "It's either me checking you out or a trip to the ER. Your choice."

Who knows what she would have done if at that very moment, Rachel hadn't appeared. Calmly assuming control as only Rachel could. It was one of the many talents Julia admired in her boss. "Gentlemen, please help Mr. Young into the salon. I've already called the police and the paramedics. Julia, come with me. We'll find something more suitable for you to wear."

Julia glanced down and silently thanked the panty gods for not letting her put on a thong that morning. The shredded hunk of fabric she'd yanked off to tend Luke had created a rather indecent slit in the front of her skirt.

"Hang on," Luke said gruffly, stubbornly

refusing to be corralled by Rafe and Jeff. "What the hell happened back there?"

"Drive-by," Rafe easily supplied. "Happens even in the good parts of town these days."

"And dogs dance," Luke responded, in no way mollified. "Wasn't there a kidnapping here a couple of weeks ago?" His voice grew louder with each word. "What kind of place are you people running that you need body-guards?"

"Remember," Julia began on a rush of breath. "There was a kidnapping here. We have a pretty high-profile clientele, so we're overly cautious."

Julia watched as Rachel mouthed the in-structions "Fix this" to Rafe before she hurried Julia into the building. The two women went upstairs, then through the expertly hidden doorway to the secret offices of Miami Confidential.

Clare, Nicole and Samantha were already seated at the long, oval conference table. Laptops whirled to life as Julia went to the closet, pulled out a pair of jeans and used the partially closed door as a privacy screen while she changed.

Rachel was already barking orders to burn copies of the exterior surveillance tapes on to disks before they turned the originals over to the local authorities. "We have to appear to be cooperating fully," Rachel reiterated. "We'll have a hard time making headway on the Botero kidnapping if this place is crawling with Miami PD.

"Now give me a damage assessment on the guy you were with," she said, her cool blue eyes trained on Julia.

"In for a fitting for the Lopez-Mitchell wedding. He doesn't have any connection to the kidnapping. Just a matter of wrong place, wrong time."

"You're forgetting wrong man," Rachel added. "Time's a-wasting, Julia. I want to know what you know before the police get here."

"Luke Young, thirty-five," Julia told her boss as she tucked in her shirt. Why was she feeling so protective of him? "Owns a commercial construction firm here in Miami. Carmen Lopez is his foster sister. Other than that, I don't know much."

One of Rachel's dark brows arched impatiently. She obviously expected every atom of truth.

Julia couldn't tell her everything. Hell,

most of the time she could barely admit it to herself. "Well, except that I left him standing at the altar six years ago."

"Kind of an important detail." Rachel scowled.

Samantha, Nicole and Clare sat silently, content to be spectators. Eight small screens, stacked in two neat rows of four, lined one portion of the wall. From her vantage point, Julia could see every inch of Weddings Your Way. She also had views of the exterior. The pool and long wooden dock jutting out into Biscayne Bay were deserted.

The street, driveway and courtyard were another matter. An ambulance came to an abrupt halt just behind Julia's Jeep. Four blue-and-white squad cars positioned themselves on either side of the ambulance. The wail of sirens cut through the stucco walls as red and blue lights spun a bright kaleidoscope of color.

"You're hurt," Rachel said.

Julia looked down at her own body, confused. "No, I'm—"

"Hurt. I want you in that ambulance with Mr. Young. I want to know every word he says and who he says it to. I want to know everything right down to the number of gauze pads they use to clean his wound."

"Rachel, the cops are going to want a statement from me," Julia countered.

"And you'll give them one just as soon as you have your injuries assessed at the hospital. Samantha, I want to know everything there is to know about Mr. Young. I want proof positive that there is no connection between him and the Botero family or Juan DeLeon." Rachel waved her hand, indicating that they should all return to the public side of the building. As she walked ahead, she continued to issue assignments. "As soon as the cops leave, I want our forensics run on any evidence. I'll call my contact at the state crime lab.

"Okay, ladies, let's make this quick and painless. Except for you, Julia. You need to be hurting."

"Got it."

A few minutes later, Julia was rubbing her side and commenting on a phantom pain in her ribs. She was careful not to ham it up too much, but she knew slipping in a small complaint about painful breathing was a guaranteed ticket into the ambulance.

Strenuous workouts made it pretty easy for her to keep her respirations shallow. The plan was sound except for Luke's reaction to her "injuries."

Her guilt was multiplying by the minute. His dark eyes never left her face, and somehow he'd managed to capture her hand in his. Completely ignoring his own very real injury, he was the picture of compassion as they sped through the early evening traffic, strapped to gurneys.

"Thank God you weren't shot," he said, squeezing her hand. "That was a brave thing you did. Brave, but damn stupid, throwing yourself at me like that."

"Well, there's gratitude for you. No good deed goes unpunished."

"You know that's not what I meant. But, my God, Julia, this could have turned out very differently...."

"Yeah. I'd rather have bruises and contusions than a big old entry wound."

He frowned, not in any way amused. "You might have a punctured lung."

"I don't." She closed her eyes. Closed him out.

Hating that she was again forced into a situation with him built on a shaky foundation of lies and misrepresentations. Especially when he seemed to be such a decent guy. "I don't want to talk for a while, okay?" she said weakly, feigning discomfort.

She thought about his heartfelt apology. Replaying his words in her mind only multiplied her self-loathing. Yes, keeping up the pretext of a hardworking seamstress in a wedding salon was part and parcel of her job. Just as playing the naive Vegas waitress had been an important part of her cover for the Esterhaus sting six years ago.

But all the rationalization in the world couldn't assuage her conscience. Not when he looked at her with genuine concern evident in his gaze. Not when he was gently stroking the back of her hand with his thumb.

The ambulance came to a sudden, jolting stop in the emergency bay of Miami General. The doors flew open and the attendants rolled their stretchers into the bright, sterile examination area.

A thin, faded curtain was drawn between them. Julia could see Luke's silhouette as he moved from the stretcher to the exam table with the assistance of a very chipper sounding nurse.

"What happened?" the woman cooed to him in a voice that practically begged, *And can I kiss it better for you?*

Julia rolled her eyes just as another nurse came into her own small cubicle—a middle-aged woman whose white shoes made squishy sounds as she maneuvered around the bed. Her black hair was pulled into a tight knot on her crown, and a pair of half-glasses rested low on her nose. "I'm Annette," she stated in a bored tone. "I need to get some information. Name?"

In less than three minutes, Julia had provided all the basic biographical and medical information, as well as a brief recap of her chief complaint. Annette, who seemed most interested in whether she had health insurance, scribbled on a form, then made her sign her name in six different places. Then she was given a gown and a thin sheet and told to change. The nurse stood at the ready with a plastic bag, shoving each article of clothing inside and labeling the bag with a marker.

"One of the docs will be in soon and then probably send you for some X-rays," Annette announced. Efficiently, she clipped a monitoring device onto Julia's fingertip, then started to leave. "Oh, and the police are here. Want me to send them in?"

Julia nodded, thinking she might as well get it over with. She was distracted when the curtain separating her from Luke fluttered. Her eyes fixed on his outline.

Apparently his nurse thought he needed help removing his shirt. *Yeah, right.* Julia could almost hear the other woman drooling as she "assisted" Luke in guiding the shirt over the cut on his head.

"If you get dizzy, feel free to use me for balance," the nurse suggested.

Or sex, Julia added cattily.

"My name's Toni, by the way."

And I dot the I with a little happy face.

"We're pretty slow right now, so I can stay with you until the doctor is available. Just in case you need anything."

Like me. When had she turned into a jealous woman? Luke was a handsome man. A man who didn't belong to her. He was business.

Luke barely noticed the young nurse buzzing around his bed. He was more interested in Julia. He felt the cool air against his chest as he sat on the edge of the thin mattress, straining to see her through a crack between the curtain and the tiled wall. The smell of alcohol and antiseptic was strong and he had the beginnings of a killer headache.

The incessant sound of some machine beeping wasn't helping. The nurse pressed a small ice pack against his scalp, then guided his hand to hold it in place.

"You should lie back."

"I'm fine," Luke insisted. "Can we open the curtain?"

The nurse's hopeful smile slipped. "Oh, right. She came in with you?"

He nodded and was punished with a dull thud of pain at the base of his skull. "Is she okay?"

The nurse shrugged. "I'm sure she'll be fine."

"Why don't I see for myself?" he asked pointedly. The nurse was sidetracked by the appearance of a short, nerdy looking guy wearing green scrubs and a too-large white coat.

"I'm Dr. Hallabach."

"Luke Young."

The doctor had Luke remove the ice pack, then did a quick examination of the wound. "It could probably use a stitch or two. Or I can close it with surgical glue and a butterfly bandage. Your call."

"Glue," Luke answered without hesitation. "I love that stuff." He thought it wise to keep to himself his own first-aid technique of using Crazy glue on a wound.

The doctor flipped through his chart. "Yes, I see you've been in here often enough to be considered a frequent flyer."

"Goes with the job," Luke said, expelling his breath.

"Did you fall at work?" he asked as he opened a drawer and brought out a prepackaged kit of everything needed to close the cut.

"Nope. I was shot at," he admitted candidly.

The doctor responded with a dry smile. "Well, that explains why the cops are waiting to talk to you." He had Luke shift around so he could work. "We should probably get a series of head films," he said a few minutes later as he snapped off his latex gloves. "And we've got to be concerned about a concussion."

"I'll take a pass on the X-rays. And I've had a few concussions over the years, so I know the drill," Luke assured the doctor. The faster this guy left, the sooner he could get a look at Julia and make sure she was okay. "Thanks, doc."

"All the same, I'll have the nurse give you a form on potential complications. Need anything for pain?"

"I'm good." Luke was already shoving himself off the mattress.

"Stay put," Hallabach instructed. "I'll let the officer know you're all set."

Luke grabbed the doctor's arm, halting his exit. "How's the lady in the next room?"

"Don't know. I can check."

"Thanks."

As soon as the doctor left, Luke grabbed his shirt. He was just about to yank open the curtain when he heard the static of the approaching policeman's radio, and his whole body tensed.

Julia was restless and worried. Because of her own deceit, she was trapped waiting for pointless tests. Her doctor was a really thorough woman who seemed determined to find the cause of Julia's phantom breathing difficulties.

On top of that, she had just spent the better part of a half hour recapping the shooting at Weddings Your Way to an officer. Julia was careful not to divulge too much. Though the Miami PD was excellent, she had a personal and professional stake in finding Sonya. As well-intentioned as they might be, she wasn't about to risk her friend's safe return—and she refused to even consider the possibility of the alternative—on the constraints that limited law enforcement. Miami Confidential was effective in part because they didn't have to obtain warrants or worry about other cumbersome legalities. There'd been many times when she was with the DEA that some scumbag had gone free due to a technicality. Now that wasn't a concern.

But Luke was. A big one, since he was about to be released.

Slipping off the bed, Julia inched closer to the curtain. She was just about to yank it open when she realized the police officer had stepped into the adjacent treatment area.

"Mr. Young?" the officer asked rhetorically. "Sergeant Lindstrom, Miami PD."

Flattening herself against the wall, Julia leaned to the side, straining to hear the muffled conversation as she took her finger and very slowly moved the fabric in order to create a small opening, allowing her to see both men. She held her breath and listened to hear the quiet tone presumably being used to maintain privacy.

"Can you tell me what happened?"

Luke shrugged, and her attention momentarily diverted from their conversation to the outline of his broad shoulders. He sat on the edge of the exam bed, his jean-clad legs spread, construction boots almost touching the floor. His torso was deliciously bare, his skin satin smooth, and bronzed from hours in the sun. Julia's mouth watered.

The man definitely had a great body. She

could just make out the faint ripple of his chest muscles. Even sitting, he towered over the officer, dwarfing the other man by a good four inches. But it was the odd expression on his face that brought her back from her inappropriate musings.

It was a hard, stoic look she'd never seen him wear before. Not angry, exactly, but something definitely had his shorts tied in a knot.

"So," the officer prodded as he moistened a fingertip and flipped through the pages of a small notepad. "Ms. Garcia indicated that the shots were fired from a black sedan parked on the street."

"Then Ms. Garcia saw more than I did. We were walking, then I was flat on my ass and bullets were flying."

"So, you're saying that you have no idea who fired the shots?"

"Yes. Right. Don't have a clue." He hooked his thumbs into the belt loops at the back of his waistband in a gesture she realized was due to nerves. Carefully hidden. But Julia was used to summing people up in a glance. Luke was hiding something. That or telling a lie. She frowned, scanning his features as he talked to the officer.

Why was Luke so uncomfortable, when he was basically telling the cop that he didn't know a thing?

Her brows drew together as she contemplated his body language. Luke, who was normally relaxed, seemed as tense as he had, well, as he had on their wedding day. She'd put it down to nerves then, too. He slid off the table and pulled his bloodstained T-shirt over his head.

"I ran a background check on you, Mr. Young," the officer was saying. "Are you sure you don't want to rethink that answer?"

The two men eyed one another like predators sizing up prey.

Luke tugged his shirt down to cover his washboard abs, then ran both hands—very carefully, Julia noticed—through his hair. Nerves, absolutely. But why?

He said, "Yeah, I'm sure."

The policeman shoved his hat back on his forehead, revealing about an inch of a neatly trimmed, blond brush cut and a swath of paler skin. His eyes, which were a watery shade of blue, narrowed accusingly. "I have a hard time believing that based on the information I received on you."

"Sorry you're having a hard time," Luke

said tightly, straightening his T-shirt in his waistband. "But like I said, there's nothing I can add to your investigation."

"The doctor says you're good to go. So I'll need you to come to the station house with me."

Julia's stomach clenched.

"Why?" Luke asked.

She heard a lot of contempt, and possibly resignation, in that single syllable.

The officer spread his feet. "Because shots were fired at you, and you're a convicted murderer. Let's go."

Chapter Four

Leaning against her Jeep in the police station parking lot, Julia fixed her attention on the door of the large art deco building cattycorner to the street. A gentle breeze danced over her skin as dusk painted the sky a soft palette of turquoise, coral and pink.

The climate was one of the main reasons she was glad to be back in south Florida. There was something familiar and soothing about the sound of palm fronds swaying overhead and the hint of salt in the air. Those few minutes before the sun slipped away were her favorite time of day.

She shoved her sunglasses up on her head, using them as a headband as she waited. The stunning sky was a nice distraction from her impatience. Standing idle wasn't her strong suit. Especially not when she had about a million questions, and the only man who could provide the answers was still inside the police station.

It took another hour before Luke, looking nettled and gorgeous, slammed out of the double glass doors. His strides were long and purposeful until he glanced up and noticed her.

She hoped she looked a lot more casual than she felt.

Luke's expression softened as their eyes met, which only heightened the heavy burden of Julia's guilt. Hiding behind a forced smile, she waved him over to where she'd parked beneath a streetlamp.

"How are you feeling?" He bracketed her arms with his hands. Concern etched deep lines on either side of his eyes as he looked down at her. "I was so worried I was ready to use my one phone call to check on you."

Her heart did a little hop, skip and jump as she tilted her head back to meet his gaze. "I'm fine. I just got the wind knocked out of me."

A current sparked in the foot or so separating them, zapping her where his callused palms pressed against the bare flesh of her upper arms. The subtle scent of his cologne tickled her already overloaded senses and her throat felt tight. With longing—no, *guilt*, she reminded herself.

Her gaze dropped to his mouth. Big mistake. Her skin tingled with the memory of his last kiss and a sudden, strong urge for the next one.

She didn't remember the last time her body had come alive with awareness. Actually, she did. It was six years ago, when Luke had pulled her into the elevator and kissed her until her legs had literally buckled. Time had managed to intensify the attraction between them, making it even stronger than she remembered. So this physical awareness of Luke wasn't new. She'd felt it as strongly all those years ago. But somehow the attraction she felt for this man seemed more intense this time around. She had no idea why he affected her the way he did. But it was as disconcerting as it was thrilling.

His hands slipped away as he stepped back from her. She experienced an odd sense of abandonment as the physical connection was broken. "What are you doing here?" he asked, glancing around the almost empty lot before looking at her again. He'd reined himself in. Turned off some sort of emotional switch.

Nice trick, and one Julia had struggled to perfect herself over the years.

"Your SUV is still at Weddings Your Way," she told him. "I thought you might need a ride."

His head tipped to one side as his mouth pulled into a tight, grim line. "You heard what that idiot cop said, didn't you?"

She could have lied, but didn't. "Yes."

Briefly, he squeezed his eyes shut and let out a mirthless laugh. "Well, then, I guess I have some explaining to do."

That's my assignment. "Only if you want to."

"It happened when I was a juvenile. I paid my debt to society and I was told the records were sealed. That's a chapter in my life I don't revisit." His voice roughened, and Julia read the No Trespassing sign as if it was in flashing neon.

"Whatever. Ready to go?" She turned and reached for the door handle.

"That's it?" he asked, his expression wary over the roof of the car as he rounded the Jeep and climbed into the passenger seat.

She started the engine and buckled her seat belt. "I came to give you a ride. I figure you've had enough interrogating for one day." *This* day, anyway.

"That's decent of you."

Not really. "It's no big deal."

"Sure it is. Unless there's some hidden agenda."

He was quick, she'd give him that. "The agenda," she told him coolly, "was to give you a ride." She gripped the wheel a little more tightly. "I can turn around and take you back to the parking lot to fend for yourself if you'd prefer."

"No," he said emphatically, angling in the seat so that she felt his eyes boring into her profile. "Why would you come within fifty feet of me after the cop mentioned my conviction? I wouldn't have pegged you as the prison pen pal type."

"Self-interest," she said evasively. "Carmen heard about the shooting and called the salon. I told her you were giving your statement and everything was fine." She'd been curious about what Carmen knew concerning her foster brother, even thought about asking, but the timing was wrong.

"Thanks for covering my butt. Now tell my why."

Talk about a dog with a bone. Luke wasn't a stupid man, and she wondered just how long she'd be able to keep up the pretext of an innocent bystander. "I told you, Weddings Your Way prides itself on customer satisfaction. We don't want one of our brides having a complete meltdown because her brother was caught in a drive-by. *Especially* when said drive-by happened on our street."

"Not on your street," Luke countered. "In your driveway. The cops think it was related to that socialite kidnapping. Once they figured out there isn't a reason in hell that I'd be a target, they crawled all over me trying to find some connection between me and the Botero family."

"Is there one?"

"Hardly," he snorted. "I'm a blue-collar guy. The closest I've ever come to Carlos Botero or his daughter is reading about them in the newspaper. We don't exactly travel in the same social circles."

"That isn't completely true," she said hesitantly, armed with the background information gathered by the Miami Confidential team. "You did some work on the Botero estate a few years ago, didn't you?"

"You and the cops," he groaned, slapping his hand on his thigh. "I was one of a few hundred guys who worked on the renovation. And it wasn't a few years, it was a decade ago."

There were several seconds of ragged breathing, then he asked, "How do you know that?"

"I know the Boteros."

"You do?"

This was the one topic about which she could be completely honest, and it felt surprisingly good. "My dad died when I was in high school. The Botero family took me in."

"Wow."

"*Big* wow," she readily agreed. "My dad was their landscaper. I was a scholarship student at the same school as Sonya and we'd become good friends. When the state threatened to ship me off to a group home, Uncle Carlos stepped in."

"Good for you. The foster care system sucks."

"It isn't the ideal situation," Julia agreed. "But not all foster homes are bad."

"A lot of them are."

"I take it you didn't have a good experience."

She heard him expel a deep sigh. "I got bounced around pretty good."

"But you got a sister out of it, right?" Julia asked as emotion squeezed at her heart. "Carmen is very, very sweet."

"She's a doll," Luke agreed. "I just hope she's happy with Dalton the Third. She deserves it."

"Do you have reservations?"

"Of course. They're from different worlds. I only hope she fits in with his snooty family. In case you didn't notice, the Mitchell family is a collection of stiffs."

Julia pressed her lips together to keep from laughing. His description of his sister's future in-laws couldn't be more dead-on. The groom's four brothers were nearly identical clones of the character Niles from the television show *Frasier*. The sister was a little wisp of a woman with brightly bleached hair and a Botox-induced, expressionless face.

"Dalton seems like a stable man and Carmen adores him."

"That she does," Luke agreed. "He's okay, just not much of…well, a *guy*. Know what I mean?"

"He's cultured," Julia offered, though her defense lacked enthusiasm. Dalton was a little too polished and mannered for her tastes. Not that those were bad qualities; she just liked men who were more hands-on.

"He's a wuss," Luke said candidly. "A nice wuss, but the guy probably sleeps in a jacket and tie. I don't trust a man who doesn't own a pair of jeans."

Julia had a feeling Luke didn't trust people, period. She'd read the hastily collected dossier prepared by Miami Confidential. The man had a lot of acquaintances but few, if any, friends. Aside from Carmen—who wasn't talking—no one seemed to know much more than superficial facts about Luke's life.

Julia turned at the stop sign, then parallel parked on the street in front of Weddings Your Way. After cutting the engine, she reached for the door handle. She froze when Luke's large hand closed over her thigh. The unexpected feel of his touch trapped her breath in her chest.

His face was hidden in shadows, making it impossible for her to get a read on the situation.

"Yes?"

"We've both had a lousy day. What do you say we go grab some dinner?"

"Your head is glued together. Shouldn't you go home and get some rest?"

"I've had worse hangnails," he joked. "Unless, of course, I can wrangle a pity meal out of it, in which case it hurts like hell."

"Having dinner with you is probably a really bad idea." Except that the alternative was walking into the office and admitting that she hadn't gotten any information out of Luke.

"Food is never a bad idea," Luke insisted, punctuating the invitation with a gentle squeeze to her knee. He sensed she was vacillating, so he pressed harder. "Consider it my way of thanking you for saving my life."

"Okay. But just so we're clear, we're going off in search of nourishment. Nothing else."

He chuckled. "I'll be a regular Boy Scout."

They got out of the car and Julia suggested a small restaurant around the corner, an easy walk. As she rounded the Jeep, stuffing her keys into the front pocket of her jeans, she asked, "Were you ever a Boy Scout?"

"No. But I did have a fight with a kid in a Cub Scout uniform when I was seven. Does that count?"

She smiled. "Not unless you got a badge for it, no."

He fell into step with her, liking the way her heeled sandals clicked against the pavement. That wasn't the only thing he liked. Not by a long shot.

Her ebony hair was an unruly mass of perfect curls that framed her face. He knew exactly what it felt like to tangle his fingers in those silky tresses. It was heaven. Remembering was also weird as hell.

He'd often thought about that week in Vegas and pretty much consigned it to nothing more than a minor break with reality. Had they married, knowing practically zilch about one another, they would probably be divorced by now. All in all, being left at the altar had proved to be a good thing.

Well, *good* was an exaggeration. Until today, the last time he'd seen Julia, he'd been handcuffed, lying facedown on the floor of the chapel. Not exactly the way he'd wanted to be remembered. And how, Luke asked himself, was today that different than the last time he'd seen her?

He'd been shot at and hauled off to a police station.

The reunion wasn't going much better, he thought, frowning in the darkness. "We don't do very well when we're together, do we?"

She glanced over at him but kept walking. "Dinner was your idea. I don't have a problem foraging for myself."

"That's not what I meant," he stated, raking his hand through his hair. "It's just that whenever I'm around you, life tends to get a little nutty. My regular life isn't like this. I get up, I go to work, I go home. I did catch a Marlins game a few weeks ago."

"A regular party animal," Julia said with a smile in her voice. "What's your point?"

Luke resisted taking her arm as they stepped over a stray railroad tie while crossing a gravel parking lot adjacent to a small, public marina. He sensed she didn't want to be touched right now. And frankly, he was fine with that. Touching Julia was a dangerous business all around. He wanted to do more than touch. But this time he was determined to go slow and easy. Assuming there was a *this time*. Jury was still out on that. So he needed to keep his wits about him.

There was a small restaurant at the end of the dock, a typical Florida eatery. The exterior was covered with some sort of marine mural. The air was thick with an odd combination of scents—food grilling in the kitchen and diesel exhaust from idling boat motors.

"The point is, I don't want you to think my life is about guns and drugs. I've spent the last few years building my business." He stopped talking while they were greeted by a brunette waitress.

Automatically, Luke placed his hand at the small of Julia's back as they weaved through the modest dining room to a small table on the wooden deck. The last of the setting sun was a golden streak separating the blackness of the ocean and the blackness of the night sky.

Small hurricane lanterns illuminated the tables, and the sound of the surf was counterpoint to the soft murmur of the voices of other diners.

As soon as they were seated, the waitress left two menus in the center of their square patio table and promised to be back for their drink orders.

The area was well lit and nearly deserted. One other table was occupied, but that couple was several feet away and completely engrossed in their own conversation. A large speaker was mounted at the roof line, spilling steel drum music out over the deck.

Luke looked across the table and watched as Julia removed her sunglasses from the top of her head and hooked them into the front of her blouse. He swallowed as his eyes followed the path of the glasses. Blouse was a bit of a stretch. It was more like a thin layer of transparent, floral fabric that allowed him to see every stitch of the pale pink camisole clinging to her generous curves.

"Hungry?" she asked.

"Very," he admitted, shifting uncomfortably against the plastic chair. "Want a drink? Wine, something?"

"They have great Les Terrasses here. It's a red from Spain. Oh, wait." She frowned. "You probably shouldn't drink with a concussion."

It was his turn to frown. "It's not a big thing." He reached up and smoothed his hair over the now-closed gash. "In my line of work, cuts and bruises are common. Besides, I'm tough."

"Or dense," she teased.

Some of the discomfort seeped from his taut muscles when he sensed she was beginning to relax. Her smile seemed more genuine than it had earlier outside the police station. He took in a deep breath and let it out slowly as he grabbed up the menu and perused the offerings.

He was starving. And not just for nourishment. What was it about this woman that made him so nuts? Cautiously, he stole a quick glance at her over the edge of the menu. He didn't want to freak her out by staring, but he just couldn't seem to get enough of her. Each time he looked at her, his heart thudded against his ribs.

He wasn't a serial dater. He'd taken a few shots at relationships in the course of thirty-five years. None of them had had this effect on him. And he'd never screwed up any of his affairs this badly. Now he needed a way to fix it. If he wanted a fresh start with Julia—and he did—then he had to find a way to connect with her. But how?

Julia ordered wine while he opted for a beer. The faint ringing of channel markers was carried on the light breeze washing over the deck. With the temperature still lingering in the low seventies, it was a picture perfect night. Stars danced in and out as night clouds slipped by overhead. A small sliver of moon hung low near the horizon.

The waitress brought their drinks and a basket of yeast rolls that actually made Julia salivate. It was no wonder. The half bagel she'd eaten on the way into work seemed like a lifetime ago.

She was slathering butter on a roll when she glanced up and caught Luke smiling at her. "What?"

"I'm just not used to seeing a woman dive

into bread. I thought the whole world was anti-carb."

She chuckled softly. "Not me. I think food is one of life's most basic pleasures. I'm Cuban, so my DNA requires me to consume lots and lots of carbs. Black beans and rice will always be my comfort food."

"Do you cook?"

She shrugged. "I know how, but my hours don't really lend themselves to hearth and home. Besides, it's easier to just grab a meal out than cook for myself."

"You live alone?"

"Uh-huh. I had a cat once, but it ran away. You?"

Luke nodded. "Alone on my boat."

She straightened in her chair. "You build things but you don't have a home?"

"Boat's home," he replied. "It's actually very practical. A lot of my business is on or adjacent to water, so when the need arises, I can stay on site."

"What kind of boat?"

"A forty-two-foot Catalina."

Her eyes grew wide. "That's a very nice boat."

He shrugged. "It's home. I've got a futon at my office when I feel the need for dry land. Other than that, I like the solitude of being out on the water." He took a long pull on his beer, then added, "When I have time."

"Does it have a name?"

"All boats have names."

"And yours is?" she pressed.

"The *Freedom*."

"Literal or metaphorical?"

"Some of each." He looked down at the menu. "So, what's good here?"

"The dolphin is great, if you like fish."

"Dolphin it is." He closed the menu and laid it on the table. "So, how'd you learn to sew?"

"Necessity. The neighbor who watched me after school was a whiz with a needle and thread. She taught me everything she knew, so when money got tight, I took in sewing."

"How old were you?"

"Twelve."

"Didn't that violate the child labor laws or something?"

"Better than going on public assistance," Julia insisted. "It took some of the pressure off my dad. He was emphatic that I attend Catholic school. I didn't get a scholarship until high school, so the extra money I made helped with tuition and uniforms."

His expression grew more serious. "Is that why we didn't sleep together?"

Julia decided that the more she shared, the better chance she had at prying information from him. "As I recall, you were the one who put the brakes on."

He offered up a sheepish grin. "One of many foolish decisions I've made over the years. At the time, I thought it was an appropriate way of proving that I wasn't using you."

She struggled to keep her expression neutral as a fresh wave of guilt washed over her. This situation would be a whole lot easier if Luke wasn't such a decent person. "I never thought you were."

The waitress arrived with two platters of blackened dolphin, sliding the dishes onto the table with practiced ease. She looked at Luke and asked, "Can I get you folks anything else?"

"We're fine, thanks," he answered, his smile polite but impersonal.

Julia watched the effect his casual grin had on the waitress. As soon as the woman was out of earshot, she said, "That smile of yours is a pretty powerful weapon."

"Not very effective on you."

Wrong. "It doesn't have to be. This…" she paused and wagged her finger back and forth between them "…isn't going anywhere."

His brows drew together and he grew pensively quiet for a few long seconds. "So, what's it going to take for me to get a second date with you?"

She locked her gaze with his. "This isn't a date, remember?"

"Dinner, candlelight," he countered easily. "Sure feels like a date."

"Well, it isn't. We're eating together because we were both hungry. The candles are citronella to keep the mosquitoes at bay, not for ambiance."

"I don't remember you being this difficult."

Julia swallowed a bite of food. "That's because we didn't ever take the time to get to know one another."

"I've learned a lot tonight. I know you've worked your way up from humble beginnings. I know about the Boteros. See, we're making progress."

This was her opening. "*You're* making progress. All I know about you is that you live on an expensive boat."

Luke's fork stilled in midair. "Don't be

too impressed. The bank owns most of the boat. Or at least they will for the next five years."

"I stand corrected."

They ate in relative silence. Julia's appetite waned after about the third bite. As much as she didn't want to, she needed to find a way past Luke's defenses. The thought of returning to Weddings Your Way with nothing of substance wasn't very appealing. Rachel expected results, and if Julia had any hopes of moving up in the Confidential organization, now was the time.

Except, she thought as she glanced across the table, it meant deceiving this man for a second time.

"It's about what that cop said, right?"

"Excuse me?" she asked, abandoning her half-finished meal.

After polishing off his beer, Luke placed the bottle on the table and lifted his eyes to hers. "Dinner tomorrow night."

"Still not following," she admitted, uncrossing and recrossing her legs and securing her napkin under the edge of her plate.

"I'll give you the short version of my past if you'll agree to have dinner with me tomorrow night."

Play it cool. "What makes you think I'm that curious about you?"

"This," he said as he reached out and brushed his fingertips along her arm.

Julia's skin tingled and her breath caught audibly. *So much for cool.* She jerked her arm away from his hand and pressed her lips together.

Luke responded with a knowing, satisfied grin. "Do you know that your lashes flutter when I touch you?"

"I'm not used to being touched."

He leaned forward and said, "I'd be happy to remedy that."

A bolt of white-hot desire shot through her. "P-pass, thank you." She'd probably go straight to hell for all this lying, Julia thought, pushing her plate away an inch just for something to do.

He seemed undeterred by her rejection. "Okay. I'll up the ante. If I tell you about my sordid past *and* promise not to touch you unless you specifically ask, will you have dinner with me tomorrow night?"

"Hands off, explain that whole conviction thing and then I'll *consider* having dinner with you."

He chuckled softly. "Deal."

Julia was forced to wait while the server delivered drink refills and cleared the table. "So, what's your deep dark secret?" she asked, trying not to sound as impatient as she felt.

His expression grew hard and his eyes fixed on the dark water beyond the pier. "My mother died when I was a baby. My grandmother was awarded custody."

"Then how did you end up in foster care?"

"Granny was a flaming alcoholic. I guess my teacher ratted her out to DCF. Next thing I know, I'm living with a bunch of strangers."

Julia remembered how she'd felt when the same possibility had loomed in front of her all those years ago. She thanked God for the Boteros. "How old were you?" she asked softly.

"A week shy of six."

Her heart clenched at the mental image of a small child being yanked from his home. Torn from anything familiar. Anything safe. Granted, it was for his protection and safety, yet it was still a scary thing for a kid. "That must have been rough."

His broad shoulders lifted in a shrug, straining against his soft cotton shirt. Julia hated that, in the midst of him telling her a horrific tale, she noticed the impressive outline of his biceps. A reminder that she'd better keep her thoughts pure and her mind on her job.

"Yeah, well, I had some *adjustment* issues," he admitted with a humorless smile. "Got me bounced through a half-dozen foster homes. I landed with the Andersons when I was fifteen."

"Was that where you met Carmen?"

He nodded, his expression noticeably softened. "Yep. She was eleven and we bonded pretty quickly. The Andersons had one biological child and he wasn't exactly thrilled to be sharing his home with a bunch of rejects from the group home."

"Sounds unpleasant."

"It wasn't great. It was easier for me—I was pretty hardened by then. Carmen was shy and insecure, so it was harder for her. A.J. was too young to know any better."

"A.J.?"

"The third foster kid. He works for me now."

"That's nice of you."

"Jury's still out on that one. After everything happened, A.J. had a tough time of it. I'm hoping this time he'll stay away from drugs and get his life together." Luke took a long pull on his beer.

"I hear guilt in your voice," she said, reading the flash of raw emotion in his eyes.

"I can't help but think things would have been different if…"

She waited, but he didn't say anything. When several protracted seconds passed and she couldn't stand the unfinished sentence in the air, she asked, "What? Different if what?"

"If I hadn't killed my foster father."

Chapter Five

Her eyes widened, but to her credit, Julia didn't run shrieking from the restaurant. Luke told himself that was a good thing. "It wasn't intentional," he said dryly.

"One would hope not." Her tone was light, but he read interest and, yes, compassion in her pretty gray eyes. "A crime of passion?"

"Yeah, I *passionately* thought he needed his ass kicked."

He watched, transfixed, as she lifted the wineglass to her smiling lips and took a sip. Her mouth was an invitation. Luke longed for another taste, remembering vividly the soft feel of his mouth on hers. Six years had done little to quell his attraction to this woman.

Before his thoughts landed squarely in the gutter, he decided to put it all out there. "I'd be lying if I said I was sorry the old bastard is dead."

"What happened?"

Luke was taken aback by the casual ease of her question. No fear, no repulsion, no condemnation. Not the reaction he'd expected. Either she was the most unflappable woman to ever walk the planet, or she hid her feelings like a pro. He wondered what past experiences she was drawing on to remain *this* detached to his admission that he'd killed someone. "I hit him." Hard. God. "Frank fell back, fractured his skull and died a week later." *And God help me,* Luke thought, *I was* glad. *Scared out of my mind, but so damn relieved that he would never come near anyone. Not ever again.* He flattened his clenched fist on the tablecloth, forcing his fingers to relax.

"I was charged with manslaughter," he told Julia unemotionally. "Tried as a juvenile and spent five years incarcerated." His muscles tensed as he braced himself. Surely she'd react in some predictable way now that she'd heard and digested his condensed— albeit incomplete—version of the facts.

The candlelight danced in her eyes, but other than that, there was nothing. Nothing. Man, he'd hate to play poker with Julia—it was impossible to get a read on her tranquil expression. He wondered just how tranquil she'd be if he told her an *unedited* version of the story. It was tempting, but impossible. He'd given his word.

As the seconds ticked by, he felt the knot in his stomach tighten. He couldn't stand the silence. "No comment?" he prodded, taking his bottle with him as he leaned back in his seat. "No curiosity about why I went after Frank?"

She shook her head. "I'm sure you had a reason."

He quietly studied her guarded features. This wasn't adding up. He'd just shared a pretty ugly episode in his life and she hadn't so much as blinked. "You're pretty accepting."

"What do you want, Luke? Judgment? Absolution? Neither my job nor my place."

His gaze dropped to where she ran her fingertip around the rim of her glass. Her nails were painted a subtle shade of coral, accenting her rich, bronzed skin tone. They were trimmed to a functional length, probably in deference to all the handwork she did at Weddings Your Way. The more time he spent with her, the more confused and intrigued he became. Julia was a mass of interesting contradictions. She had a steely strength that even her stunning beauty couldn't dilute.

"You're okay with that aspect of my past?"

Just as she opened her mouth to answer, the cell phone clipped to her waistband began to vibrate. She offered an apologetic smile as she checked the number of the incoming caller.

Her heart skipped when she saw the name scroll across the display. Flipping the clam-shell-shaped phone open, she practically shouted her fears into the mouthpiece. "Uncle Carlos? Is everything—"

A deep, masculine voice cut in. "This is Sean Majors."

"What's happened?" she demanded, bracing herself for bad news. The head of security for the Botero family didn't make social calls. "Is it about Sonya? Have they—"

"It's Mr. Botero. Can you meet me at Miami General?"

The chair tumbled backward as she shot to her feet. "Miami General? What happened?"

With the phone still at her ear, she mouthed "I'm sorry" to Luke, deserting him as she moved quickly toward the door. "Sean! What's happened?"

"The paramedics think it was a mild stroke."

"Oh, God," she groaned, pushing the door open and stepping outside. "How bad?" she demanded, striding down the street, then to her car, deactivating the locks as she approached the Jeep.

"It was minor and he's going to pull through, but he's asking for you."

She rammed her keys in the ignition, grinding the engine. "I'm on my way."

Ignoring most traffic laws, Julia reached the hospital in under ten minutes. After parking illegally in a space reserved for physicians only, she sprinted into the reception area. An elderly volunteer sat behind the U-shaped desk, the top of her heavily teased, blue-gray hair barely visible above the counter.

"May I help you?"

"Carlos Botero?" Julia said quickly. "He was just brought in."

"Are you family?"

"Yes. I'm his…daughter," Julia lied impatiently.

Her attitude didn't impress the woman. It took what felt like an hour for her to hunt and peck her way across a keyboard. The tip of Julia's foot drummed against the tile floor as the woman adjusted a pair of half-glasses hanging from a beaded chain around her neck.

"He's still in Emergency. Follow the red stripe of tape on the flo—"

Julia muttered her thanks, then jogged along the sometimes-missing tape, making enough wrong turns to feel like a rat negotiating an unfamiliar maze.

After locating the ER, she spent another half minute finding Carlos. Seeing him lying in the bed, his face pale, machines flashing and bleeping, was a shock. He was a robust, commanding man. Larger than life. Or at least that's how Julia had always seen him.

Rushing to his side, she stroked his thick shock of white hair and bent down to brush a gentle kiss against his forehead. "It's Julia," she whispered. "I'm here."

He struggled to open his eyes, then offered a weak smile. She bit her lip, seeing the sluggish muscles on the right side of his face.

"Not…as…bad…as…looks." The words came out as a slurred, gravelly stream of syllables.

"Shush," Julia soothed, smiling down at him. She didn't know a lot about strokes, but she guessed the fact that he was coherent and could speak were both excellent signs. Relief washed over her. "You scared me."

"Sonya," he croaked, his eyes conveying both fear and urgency. "N…n…need—"

Julia felt a hand close on her elbow, and she glanced over her shoulder and found Sean. For a large man, he was pretty stealthy. He was tall, clean cut, with brown hair and piercing teal-green eyes. And he smelled like bubble gum.

"My daughter's shampoo. We were in the middle of bath time when I got the call," he explained before she'd even asked. "Let's step outside."

After kissing Carlos one more time, Julia followed Sean into an alcove down the hall. The bright, overhead lights were harsh, as was the pungent smell of antiseptic. The din of dozens of different conversations blended with the incessant chatter from the PA system.

"What happened?" she asked, keeping her voice down.

"Cook paged me. She was pretty hysterical. When I got to the estate, I found him unconscious in the study. The paramedics responded quickly. The doc says he'll need some rehab, but the prognosis should be positive."

"Should be?"

Sean reached into the breast pocket of his jacket and pulled out a piece of paper sealed in a plastic evidence bag. "I think this is what caused the stroke. Cook said it came just after dinner. Reading it must have sent his blood pressure through the roof."

Snatching the bag, Julia swallowed hard as she read the words:

THE PRICE IS TWO MILLION. I WILL BE IN TOUCH. IF YOU IN- VOLVE THE AUTHORITIES SHE WILL DIE. IF YOU DO NOT FOLLOW INSTRUCTIONS SHE WILL DIE.

About halfway down the page she spied a reddish-brown oval. On closer inspection, she realized it was the smear of a bloody fingerprint. A chill danced along her spine, sending a shiver through her core.

"We should find out if this is Sonya's blood," she said, her attention on the note as she scanned it for any possible clue visible to the naked eye. Other than the bloodstain she couldn't see anything. "Can I borrow this for a few hours? I have a friend who works in the pathology lab at the M.E.'s office. She'll test this quickly and discreetly."

Sean scoffed. "No way. I know you mean well, Julia, but I'm better equipped to handle this sort of thing."

Want to bet? Julia was completely frustrated. She couldn't tell Sean about Miami Confidential and yet her team had the best resources to do fast and accurate testing on the note. Talk about being caught between a rock and a hard place.

Her eyes darted around the hallway as she tried to think of a way she could liberate the note from Sean. Nothing jumped out at her. Then she spied a ladies' room five feet away.

The bagged note was still in her hand when she set her improvised plan in motion by feigning sudden weakness in her legs. She clutched at Sean's arm. Then she said, "I keep seeing Sonya in my mind's eye, scared, hurt or worse."

Sean offered a comforting smile. "We'll get her back."

"First Sonya, now Uncle Carlos. I, well, I just feel physically ill." Dramatically, she began to fan herself with the note. "My head is spinning. I think I need a glass of water."

Sean took her by the shoulders and eased her against the cool tile wall. Obviously, he wasn't going to run off to the nearest nurse's station.

"Lean back and take deep breaths," he

suggested, sounding very much like the single father that he was. "It'll pass."

Time to ratchet it up a notch. "I think I'm going to be sick," she whined. Puffing out her cheeks, she pretended to gag, then made a mad dash for the ladies' room.

She closed and locked the door before Sean could follow her inside. He did knock, but stopped when Julia made some loud sound effects to bolster the charade.

First, she pulled one of those seat liners from the dispenser on the wall. Cringing, she figured this wasn't the best situation for non-contamination while gathering evidence, but hey, it was her only option.

Taking a specimen cup from the ledge above the sink, Julia ignored the strong stench of cherry deodorizer and placed the small plastic container and the note on the sterile liner. Tugging the toilet tissue free from the wall, she separated the roller and removed the spring. She tore open a single use alcohol wipe—also courtesy of the well-stocked bathroom—and swabbed the coil.

Gingerly, she unsealed the plastic bag holding the note, being careful to use her knuckles to prevent getting any of her own fingerprints on the paper.

Her brows knit in concentration as she used the coil to scrape a minute amount of blood from the note, then made fake gagging sounds to keep Sean at bay. Tiny flecks of dried blood floated into the specimen cup. Then she hit a snag.

While she resealed the note inside the bag, she wondered how she'd get the cup out of the bathroom without Sean seeing it. As she contemplated that complication, she ran water from the faucet to mask the sounds when she put everything back into place.

Grabbing a half-dozen rough, brown paper towels from the dispenser, she dampened them with water, then carefully wrapped the container inside the layers. She checked her reflection in the mirror, making sure nothing damning showed through the damp towels. Lastly, she pinched her cheeks, making them look suitably flushed, before she held the paper towels to the nape of her neck.

"Perfect," she whispered, pleased that the jury-rigged compress looked so convincing.

With note in hand, she paused long enough to use her foot to flush the toilet, then exited the bathroom.

Sean's green eyes narrowed as he snatched the note from her, then asked, "Are you okay?"

Nodding weakly, she did a little exaggerated swallow. "I'm sorry, I guess all this is just too much for me."

"I've posted two men on Mr. Botero. I have already contacted a private lab. I'd like to get this note to them ASAP." He paused and did a cursory examination of the ransom note.

Julia held her breath. Sean was a very capable man, and she had a fifty-fifty chance that he'd pick up on her tampering. If he suspected anything, it didn't show. *Thank God.*

"They're doing some tests to assess the damage from the stroke, so you might want to think about going home."

"I'll stay for a while."

"Suit yourself," Sean said with a shrug. "As soon as the doctor is finished with him, they're moving Mr. Botero to a private room on the third floor."

"I'll see that he gets settled in," Julia promised.

She counted to fifty as soon as she saw Sean exit the hospital. Then she called Rachel from her cell.

"Brennan."

"A ransom note was delivered to the estate." Her boss muttered a curse. "Bring it here." Julia explained the situation, including her bathroom CSI moments, then added, "Can you send someone to Miami General to pick up the sample?"

"Consider it done," Rachel said. "Good work, Julia. Great job of thinking on your feet. How's Mr. Botero?"

"It was a mild stroke. I'll know more after I speak to his doctors."

"What about Mr. Young? Did you get anything out of him?"

Julia's mind flashed to how she'd abandoned Luke in the restaurant. The look on his face had been priceless—a combination of shock and curiosity. "Nothing to connect him to the shooting, so I'm thinking it had something to do with Sonya's kidnapping."

Rachel didn't respond immediately. When she did, it was in a clipped tone laced with a twinge of censure. "Nothing but a murder conviction."

Squeezing her eyes shut, Julia winced. "He mentioned it."

"When were you planning to share with the group?"

"As soon as I get more details," Julia lied. "At this point, all I know is the charges were knocked down to manslaughter. It's irrelevant anyway. It happened almost twenty years ago."

"I know, I'm looking at a copy of his sealed juvie records. Seems your Mr. Young had several brushes with the law."

"When he was a kid," Julia argued with a ferocity that surprised even her. Blowing out a frustrated breath, she backed up and tried again. "He was an angry kid batted around in the foster care system. Has he been in any trouble since then?"

"Other than the Esterhaus thing you two were involved in, nothing's turned up. So far."

"I'll call my DEA contact. Maybe Esterhaus is reaching out from prison for a little retribution."

"Rafe's already on it. If it was Esterhaus, he could have been aiming for you," Rachel said.

"Unlikely," Julia countered. "I testified in complete anonymity. The trial judge didn't even know who I was."

"Still, it's worth a look."

"There's a copy of the file in the safe at my apartment. As soon as I leave here, I'll swing by and get it."

"Stay alert," Rachel cautioned.

"Always. By the way, have you gotten the phone records from Sonya's apartment yet? My gut tells me there's something hinky about that Ramon guy."

"Should have them by morning," Rachel said. "Still working on the code to access her voice mail."

Julia had a lightbulb moment. "Try ten-four-nineteen-sixty-one."

"Which is?"

"Jon Secada's birthday. Sonya was a big fan. It's worth a try."

"Will do. I paged Rafe. He should be at the hospital in about an hour."

"Have him call my cell. I'll meet him in the parking lot. We've got to fly under the Botero security radar."

After hanging up the phone, Julia went up to check on Carlos and speak with his treating physicians. With that done, she crept into his room, relieved when she saw that he was sleeping. The dim lighting made his grayish pallor seem worse, but the doctors had assured her that his prognosis was good.

As she sat at his bedside, her thoughts drifted back to Luke. It was hard to reconcile the knowledge that he was a convicted killer. It didn't jibe with the gentle, easygoing man she was coming to know. The man a part of her wanted to love but couldn't. Not now, probably not ever.

Frowning, she reminded herself that she didn't really know him. Not that her lack of knowledge kept her from lusting after him in a big way.

During their dinner, she'd spent more than a little time distracted by his ruggedly handsome good looks. His golden, tanned skin testified to his hands-on attitude in his profession, another perk being his awesome body. The guy was in good shape.

"*Great* shape," she amended in a whisper, feeling a definite tingle in the pit of her stomach. Not that he was muscle-bound or anything. His body was more like a hard, toned sculpture—a detail she'd picked up when she'd knocked him to the ground as the bullets flew overhead.

The guilt returned. Rubbing her face, she felt the heavy burden of her deception settle on her shoulders. If the shooting was retribution for the Esterhaus thing, it was her fault. If it was related to Sonya's kidnapping, it was her fault. Bottom line was she'd put him in physical danger. Again.

Her phone began to vibrate, pulling her

out of her funk. She kissed Carlos, scribbled a note for him on the pad from the bedside table, then slipped quietly from the room.

She had the pilfered blood sample cupped in her palm as she bid the two security guards good night. Seeing their tree trunk size necks and boulderlike biceps gave her comfort. A Sherman tank would have a tough time getting past them, which suited her just fine. At least Carlos would be safe.

Stepping outside, she sucked in the clean, fresh air. It was a welcome change from the hospital. Rafe Montoya was waiting in the shadows by her Jeep. He had dark, almost black eyes, dark hair and olive skin. Like Julia, he was a former DEA agent, though most of his time with the agency had been spent immersed in the brutal drug cartels of Bolivia. It made sense. Rafe had a guarded, menacing look that made him an effective undercover agent.

"Got a ticket," Rafe remarked, a hint of humor in his tone.

Julia shrugged. "Small price to pay."

"You'll pay it, too," he said, reaching for the container she offered. "Rachel doesn't reimburse unnecessary expenses."

"I know." She waited impatiently while

Rafe held the specimen bottle up into the slice of light from the streetlamp. "Is there a problem?"

"It's a pretty small sample."

"Best I could do." She told him how she'd obtained a scraping of the blood from the ransom note.

"That Majors guy is a pain. The last thing we need is a rent-a-cop screwing with the investigation." Contempt dripped from each word.

Julia lowered her head to hide her grin. Sean and Rafe were opposite sides of the same coin. Both men were security experts. Both were wedded to their jobs. Neither liked to lose. Sonya's kidnapping represented both failure and challenge, and had sparked something of a pissing match. Julia wasn't going to get in the middle of it.

"I'm going back to my apartment," she said, snatching the parking ticket out from under the wiper blade. "I'll grab a few hours of sleep, then meet you back at Weddings Your Way."

"I'll drop this off, then go over to the Botero estate and find out where Majors took the original note. Then I'll...*liberate* it. Maybe I'll get lucky and have an opportunity to pummel Sean Majors in the process."

"Good luck with that," Julia said with a

snicker. She knew Rafe would do no such thing. For all his bluster, he'd never do anything to jeopardize the investigation. Still, she knew he above all others felt guilty that Sonya had been kidnapped in front of Weddings Your Way. From right under their noses.

Sonya's pristine white limo had just pulled up to the curb behind one of the other clients' cars when it happened. Caroline Graham and her brother, Alex, were just leaving as Sonya got out. Then a big, black limo pulled up, two men exited and grabbed Sonya after overpowering Craig Johnson. They forced Sonya into their car and sped off, hitting Caroline, leaving her gravely injured and the driver-bodyguard in the hospital.

Now Uncle Carlos was collateral damage. Yet another casualty, Julia thought with a heavy heart as she drove along Biscayne Bay on her way back to her apartment. She'd been running on adrenaline for the better part of the long day, but now that it had leached out of her system, she felt exhausted.

Until she pulled into the parking lot and found Luke seated on the cement in front of her building. Her heart fluttered in her chest at the sight of him. A dark sedan was parked in her assigned spot. Bass from the radio pounded in the air. Normally, she would have gotten out of her Jeep and had the young men move, but given that she was the proud new owner of a parking ticket, she let it slide.

Luke was standing by the time she reached him. He was directly under the security lights, his thumbs hooked through the belt loops of his jeans. The guy had great thighs.

"How'd you find me?" she asked, stopping about a foot shy of where he stood.

"Toni."

Julia blinked, then offered a mocking little grin. "The nurse?"

He nodded. "It took a little persuading, but she finally pulled your address off your hospital chart."

"What kind of persuasion?"

"I lied," he answered with unapologetic honesty. "Told her the concussion had me all dazed and confused."

Julia peered up at him through her lashes. "And she bought that?"

"Well, that and I kinda hinted that I might be calling her in the near future."

"That is cold."

"I was desperate," he insisted. "It was either a little white lie to Annette or follow you to the hospital. I didn't want to intrude, but waiting isn't one of my strong suits. How's Mr. Botero?"

"It looks good."

There was an awkward silence, then Luke said, "I could really use a cup of coffee."

"It's late," she hedged. The thought of his presence inside her small apartment didn't seem like a smart move. Then again, he'd waited all this time, so it didn't seem right to send him away. "One cup." She pointed down the sidewalk. "I'm the last unit."

He fell into step beside her. "When was this place built?"

"The fifties, I think. It used to be a motel."

"It needs renovation."

She smiled in the darkness. "Then my rent would go up."

"True, but—" He was cut off by the sound of a car squealing out of the parking lot.

They turned in unison just as Julia's apartment exploded in a fiery ball.

Chapter Six

The secret offices of Miami Confidential were tucked away on the top floor of Weddings Your Way. There were no windows to indicate if it was night or day, but Julia's body knew to the second that it was 5:00 a.m. Exhaustion pulled at her. She'd kill for a solid eight hours sleep.

She'd settle for a cup of coffee.

"How's Mr. Young?" Rachel asked the second Julia walked into the room.

Julia fell into one of the chairs rimming the conference table, absently rubbing her shoulder. The receptionist, Vicki, appeared with a steaming mug of strong coffee, which she handed her with a sympathetic smile. Julia sent her a grateful look as she brought the near-scalding drink to her lips. The bitter liquid delivered almost an immediate jolt of much-needed caffeine.

"Need anything?" Vicki asked their boss. When Rachel shook her head, Vicki disappeared into the surveillance area adjacent to the conference room.

"The doctors insisted he stay for a few hours of observation," Julia told her boss as she held the hot mug between her palms and inhaled the fragrant steam. "Understandably, they're concerned," she said with marked understatement, "since in the past twenty hours, he's been shot at and blown up."

One of Rachel's perfect brows arched. "As have you."

Julia shrugged, struggling to keep from wincing, since the action made her bruised shoulder burn. "I'm fine," she insisted. "I signed up for this. Luke didn't."

Rachel came around from her end of the table, moving gracefully in a swirl of flowing, aqua fabric. Even though it was a few minutes shy of dawn, she looked as fresh as someone who'd had a full night's sleep, a leisurely bath and a professional makeup job.

Conversely, Julia's clothing was rumpled and grass-stained, and the stench of burned hair was enough to make her gag. *Her* burned hair, singed by the flames that had destroyed her apartment along with two other units. Thankfully, one unit was empty and the woman who lived in the other apartment had been at her boyfriend's when the place exploded.

The only person who'd been hurt was Luke. Granted, his injuries were minor, but considering the earlier wound at the back of his head, Julia was feeling like a regular Typhoid Mary.

Rachel slapped a file folder on the table in front of her, then elegantly returned to her chair. The faint smell of her perfume wafted through the air, a marked improvement over singed hair, Julia thought as she reached for the file. Inside she found official, detailed telephone records for Sonya's home and cell, as well as transcripts of the five messages retrieved from her friend's voice mail system.

"The code you suggested worked," Rachel said. "I don't know whether to thank you or Jon Secada."

"Glad it worked." Relieved, Julia took another sip of coffee. "I think Sonya and I went to a dozen of his concerts when we were in high school."

She shivered, thinking about the bloody fingerprint that had caused Uncle Carlos's stroke. Closing her eyes briefly, she refused to think about what might be happening to her friend. "What about the note? Any forensics? Anything that might tell us where she is or who has her?"

"The print is definitely Sonya's," Rachel confirmed. She must have read the pained look in Julia's eyes because she quickly added, "The sample is fresh, so that means, in all likelihood, she's still alive."

Or was alive when she'd left the print, Julia thought, then pulled herself up short. *No, damn it.* She had to think positively. *Sonya is alive. She has to be.* "From your lips…" Julia slumped into the chair and massaged the tension at her temples.

After a moment she turned back to the file, reading the entries as she sipped her coffee. Thanks to a reverse directory, all the numbers were associated with names. She recognized several calls from Sonya to and from her father, her fiancé and Weddings Your Way. There were other normal items like hair salons and most of the charitable organizations Sonya was associated with. Julia surmised the calls to Ladera were related in some way to Juan. He was in the midst of an election campaign.

She shook her head. Though she didn't know the man all that well, she admired his convictions and commitments to his native country. Ladera was a powder keg of corruption, and Juan's platform placed him squarely in the drug cartel's crosshairs.

When a specific entry near the bottom of the third page caught her eye, she held up the page to show Rachel. "What's this?"

Craning her neck, Rachel read the entry upside down. "Preprogrammed forward."

Julia met and held Rachel's gaze. "Craig Johnson had this number, or at least part of it."

"I know."

Julia's mind whirled. "Then we definitely know the guy is involved in Sonya's kidnapping." The blood in her veins began to simmer. "Someone had to get to him," Julia continued as she worked it through in her brain. "Carlos Botero would never have hired Johnson as Sonya's driver if he wasn't squeaky clean. Someone from Ladera," she reasoned.

"Except that the calls were being forwarded to a Miami number." Rachel tapped the page above the notation with her fingertip. "When you called the number from Sonya's condo, it automatically went from

Ladera back to Miami. Unfortunately, the Laderan telephone system isn't as sophisticated as ours, so we're still working on finding the person or persons who set up the forward."

Julia took one last sip of coffee, then shoved back from the table. "Craig Johnson should know."

"Which is your next assignment. Drop in on him and discreetly see if you can find out who he knows in Ladera. But be careful," Rachel warned. "We're supposed to be a confidential agency. I've had enough trouble pacifying the local police. Any more 'suspicious' incidents and it'll be hard for us to fly under their radar. Thanks to Mr. Young, you've got the perfect cover."

Julia battled back a groan. "How does Luke get me to Craig Johnson? I don't need Luke in order to sneak up there and make that slimeball tell me where Sonya is being held."

"They're in the same hospital. I want information, Julia. Don't hurt the chauffeur. Hospital security is keeping a log of Johnson's visitors. You can bypass security by signing in to see Mr. Young. Unless you have a problem with the assignment?"

Of course there's a problem. I've almost gotten the guy killed twice. Three times if I count Esterhaus. "I'm on it."

"Good," Rachel replied, though there was lingering uncertainty in those blue eyes of hers. "While we're on the topic of Mr. Young, I received an edited copy of the transcripts from his trial, and I don't know... It bothers me, as if something is...*off.*"

"Like?" Julia prodded.

"Your Mr. Young had a history of, shall we say, anger issues. So why would the state's attorney plead it down to manslaughter? Especially when Young took the stand and admitted responsibility?"

"Because he was seventeen?" Julia suggested. "He didn't go into detail with me, but the situation he described was an accident. He had a fight with Frank Anderson. He never intended to kill the guy."

Rachel's brows drew together and her mouth pulled into a stern line. "You jumped in there pretty quickly to defend a murderer. Exactly what is going on between the two of you?"

"Nothing," Julia said, meeting her boss's gaze steadily. Not a lie. But not strictly the truth, either. But one couldn't be hanged for one's thoughts.

"Let's hope so, because while I think there's something hinky about his crimes, it doesn't look as if he's connected to Sonya in any meaningful way. You know our priorities. I don't want anything to jeopardize the Botero investigation. So remember the objective here."

"I remember."

"See that you do," Rachel cautioned.

"Anything else?" At Rachel's negative, Julia rose. "I'll take a shower and sack out in the ready room for a couple of hours until visiting time."

"I'll make sure you aren't disturbed."

"Thanks." She was already disturbed, Julia thought, as she made her way to the women's bathroom on the same floor. Disturbed by her unmanageable feelings for Luke.

A few minutes later, Julia stood beneath the hot, steamy spray from the shower. It felt good to wash off the debris and grime from the explosion. Hopefully, the lavender scent would be enough to mask the stench of singed hair.

After her shower, she towel dried her hair, then flopped onto the bed against the wall in the small room kept for just that purpose. She immediately fell into a deep sleep.

Two hours later she was pinning her still

damp hair into a casual pile on her head. One of the pluses to south Florida was the acceptability of beach hair.

Grabbing a pair of white capris from her locker, she paired them with a teal baby tee and strappy sandals. A few strokes of blush and a dab of lipstick erased some of the exhaustion from her face.

Before heading back to the hospital, she filled a thermal mug with more coffee. During the drive, she called and checked on Carlos's condition, sorry he wasn't in the same hospital as Craig Johnson and Luke.

Just thinking of Luke brought a renewed sense of guilt. While she knew his injuries were negligible, and keeping him in the hospital was more precautionary than anything else, it didn't help.

Real, palpable fear coiled in her stomach when she remembered seeing him prone and motionless in the grass after the explosion. She'd been in such a rush to reach him that she'd virtually crawled over the embers to get to his side. With her heart clogging her throat, she'd felt for a pulse. He'd regained consciousness by the time the ambulance arrived, and some serious attitude when they'd insisted on taking him to the ER.

Because of him, Julia had been spared the full impact of the explosion. His large frame had taken the brunt when energy from the blast had sent them both flying into the air. Julia suffered nothing more than a bruise from landing on her shoulder.

"Can this get any worse?" she muttered as she parked in the visitors' lot, cut the engine and tucked her keys into her pocket before heading to the main entrance. It was almost 8:00 a.m., and already hot.

Unlike Miami General, Biscayne Memorial was a small facility without level-one trauma capabilities. The two-story concrete building was painted a pale lime. Royal palms surrounded the place, swaying in the soft morning breeze coming off the Intracoastal. It took her less than three seconds to spot the Miami PD surveillance van in the parking lot.

Craig Johnson was the only real witness to the kidnapping of Sonya Botero. Or at least that had been his story up to this point. The surveillance was a precaution, the detectives in charge of the case probably hoping the kidnappers would try something on Johnson. He was their best lead.

Now he was Julia's prime suspect.

She followed a trio of nurses into the building, taking another swallow of now-tepid coffee as she approached the information desk. A bored, uniformed man offered her a pat smile as he shoved a clipboard across the counter. "Who are you visiting, ma'am?"

"Luke Young," she answered. "Room 217, right?"

He checked a list clipped on a corkboard behind his chair. "Yes, ma'am." He passed her a badge with the word Visitor printed in bold, red letters. Below that, he wrote Luke's room number. "Wear that at all times," he instructed with little enthusiasm. "Take the elevator up one floor. Room's about halfway down on the left."

"Thank you."

She followed the signs to the elevators, stepping inside the confined space already occupied by a doctor and four other employees. Julia acknowledged them with a slight nod of her head.

The place was fairly active. She'd timed her arrival to coincide with the shift change. If the staff was busy briefing one another, there was less of a chance that she'd be caught interrogating Johnson.

Interrogating him wasn't really foremost

on her mind. Knowing he was involved in Sonya's kidnapping made her want to hurt him. A lot.

Thanks to Rachel's briefing, and Samantha Peters's previous visits, she knew Johnson's room was in the east wing. She glanced down the hall, seeing the sign for the stairwell. She caught just a glimpse of a doctor's white coat disappearing down the stairs before she intentionally clipped her visitor's badge backward at her waistband, then casually strolled past the nurses' station.

Johnson was her assignment, but her heart and mind wished she could check on Luke first. That just wasn't feasible. Seeing Luke, leaving to question Johnson, then returning, meant she'd have to lie to him. Again. If only things were different, she thought glibly.

Her heels clicked against the tiled floor, making her a little jittery. Finding Johnson's door closed, she slowly and silently pushed it open, then slipped soundlessly into the darkened room. The blinds were drawn, so it took a few seconds for her eyes to adjust. He was little more than a silhouette on the bed.

A lying, sniveling silhouette, she thought, her temper beginning to simmer. She remembered Sonya shrieking—a sound so loud and urgent that Julia had heard it all the way up in her office. She thought about Caroline Graham's poor body slamming into the grille of the kidnapper's car as it fled the scene. She winced as she recalled the bloody fingerprint on the note. About Carlos's stroke and the ransom demand.

She wished her assignment was to strangle Craig Johnson with his IV tubes.

Instead, she took a calming breath and went over to his bedside and gave him a little jab. Nothing.

She poked harder, wanting him to wake up so she could question him. He could sleep later.

Still nothing. "Mr. Johnson?" She waited for a response, and when one never came, she repeated his name three times, louder and louder with each attempt.

Unease broke through her irritation and she reached for his wrist. His pulse was thready. Not good. Julia ran to the window and opened the blinds, looking back toward the bed. She groaned when she saw the hypodermic needle wobbling in the man's chest.

Racing to the bedside, she pressed the call button and dashed out of the room.

Julia practically flattened herself against

the wall as the whole floor seemed to mobilize. As much as she wanted to know what had happened, she couldn't risk being caught in Johnson's room. In under a minute, buzzers were sounding and a red light just outside Johnson's door began to flash.

With the staff focused on Johnson's medical crisis, Julia went to the atrium and called Rachel. In a near whisper, she reported what had transpired. Out of the corner of her eye, she watched three men she recognized as detectives burst from the elevator. "This place is crawling with Miami PD. I can hang around, at least until Luke's released. Hopefully, I can find out what happened to Johnson."

"Do it," Rachel said, irritation in her tone. "Apparently we're not the only ones onto Johnson."

"I agree," Julia said. "Looks like he's become a liability to his partners." She held the phone away from her ear as a code was called over the intercom. "Johnson might not make it," she added.

"I've got a few contacts inside the hospital. I'll see what I can find out from here. Keep me posted."

"Will do," Julia said, flipping her phone closed and clipping it back in place.

A lone, blond nurse manned the circular station between the east and west wings of the hospital. Julia noted how she kept peering down the hall, her face scrunched with concern.

Julia wandered in her direction.

"Is there something I can help you with?" the nurse asked, reluctantly tugging her attention from the commotion down the hall.

"Luke Young?" Julia asked as she leaned closer to the nurse. "Wow, what's going on down there?"

"Patients sometimes need extra attention," she answered.

What a crock. "Seems pretty serious to me. Who are all those people gathered around? They don't look like doctors."

The nurse offered a condescending little smile. "Mr. Young is in room 217. That way." She pointed a long, tanned finger in the opposite direction. Even though she was reluctant to leave the area before knowing Johnson's prognosis, Julia headed to Luke's room. She felt a little flutter in the pit of her stomach. Not from anger, not from fear, but from desire. It was as if she'd turned into a walking, talking hormone.

Her initial exhilaration at seeing Luke

again was tempered by absolute resolve. For his own safety, Julia knew she had to stay away from him. That was the smart thing. The intelligent move.

When she opened the door, intelligence sailed right out the window. Luke was propped up in bed, gloriously, magnificently shirtless. Sunlight streamed through the window, bathing his tanned body in golden light. *Wow,* she thought, suddenly dry-mouthed. Even the burns and bruises from the explosion couldn't take away from the perfection. Her heart rate shot up just looking at him. A crisp, white sheet covered him from the toes to just above his navel, but from there on up, it was all Luke. His sculpted, perfect torso was bared and brilliant. A thick V of dark hair tapered from his chest to his waist, like a big neon sign flashing Look Here! She struggled to remember how to breathe.

Seeing his mussed hair and slightly crooked smile, Julia wasn't sure she could walk the three steps to the closest chair without keeling over on her face from pure, unadulterated lust. Luke had willingly sac-rificed himself to save her. Surely these am-plified feelings were simply a mix of attraction and appreciation. Right?

He looked up, his eyes lightening at the sight of her. "Hey," he said with a smile.

"Good morning," she murmured, stepping farther into the room, determined to hide her emotions. "You look like you feel well."

"I felt fine last night. Staying here was a complete waste of my time," he complained. Concern darkened his eyes. "How about you? Aches? Pains?"

Definitely a lot of ache. "I'm great. I'm glad you're okay."

"Sit down," he suggested, patting the bed next to where the sheet was pulled taut, hugging his thighs. "You can hang out until the doctor on call shows up."

"He may be awhile. There's a…thing with one of the patients down the hall." She approached the bed one small step at a time. "I could go get you a newspaper or something to pass the time."

His eyes met and held hers. "Actually, I do need medical attention."

The deep, hypnotic sound of his voice made her stomach flutter. "Want me to call the nurse?"

He shook his head and held out his hand. He was just far enough away that his fingertips grazed the exposed skin of her belly. Her body shivered at the contact. "You can fix it," he suggested. "It hurts here," he said, tapping his cheek.

"Want an ice pack?"

"This kind of injury should be treated with heat," he said, shifting in the bed enough so that his arm snaked around her waist, drawing her to him.

Her thighs pressed against the cool railing while the warmth of his touch spread through her whole body. His chest rose and fell rhythmically. The sheet had inched lower, revealing the dimple of his navel.

Julia swallowed. "Heat pack?"

"Lips," he told her, his voice husky and quite serious. "My injuries require moist heat. *Stat.*"

She couldn't help smiling. "Stat?" The railing between them lowered and he drew her even closer. Julia braced her hand on his chest before he could pull her over him like a blanket.

His skin was sun warmed and smooth. Beneath her splayed fingers she could feel his elevated heartbeat. It matched her own.

"It hurts right here." He tapped his jaw. "Bad. Maybe if you kiss it?" he suggested, his voice husky. The devil danced in his brown eyes. Her brain said no, but her brain was no match for the desire coursing to every one of her cells. One kiss, she told herself. Just one. She leaned over and pressed her lips just above his jawline. The faint scent of soap overpowered the antiseptic hospital smell.

When she started to pull away, Luke's grip tightened. "Not there, higher," he said, his minty breath tickling her throat.

Her breasts pressed against his arm as she rose on tiptoe to brush a light kiss on his cheekbone. As she did, his fingers on her back spread, the tips moving tauntingly over the thin fabric of her shirt, tracing the valley along one side of her spine.

"Better?" Her heart raced. Julia knew she shouldn't be doing this, but it felt right, too.

"Hmm. Maybe you'd better tend this one." He tapped his temple.

"Brain damage?" she teased, her lips already against his warm skin. His hair tickled her face, and she softly brushed it out of the way. Her fingers, ignoring her common sense, tangled in his silky hair until she cupped his head.

"You're making me crazy," he said thickly, pointing out another place for her to kiss. This time above his left eye.

Crazy about you. Her heart kicked into overdrive. But of course he was kidding. She kissed his left eye, and before he asked, his right, feeling the sweep of his short lashes against her skin.

Pupils dilated, he pointed to his mouth.

Julia kissed his chin.

He groaned in disappointment and brought his other hand up to pull out the pins in her hair.

"Help me," he said in that sexy low voice. "I'm dying here."

So was she. To hell with protocol. She dipped her head and touched his mouth with hers. Heaven.

They both opened their mouths at the same time. Heat flooded her. The heady taste of him was familiar and yet new. They'd kissed often—six years ago. But that had been business. This...this was bliss.

Julia braced her hand on his chest, locking her knees so she didn't sprawl over him. Then she sank into the taste and texture of the kiss.

When he finished the sinfully amazing exploration of her mouth, Julia didn't trust her knees not to buckle.

"Do me a favor?" he asked, leaning back into the pillows.

Kiss me again and I'll walk through fire barefooted. Twice. "Depends on the favor."

"They insisted on cutting off my clothes in the ambulance. Could you go to my boat and get me something to wear?"

Once she got over the visual of Luke naked, she realized that getting his clothes was the least she could do, given that it was her fault he'd been blown up. The memory gave her the strength to step back and clear her head. "Sure, where's the boat?"

"Costal Marina."

She blinked. "Next to Weddings Your Way? How is that possible? How did we not run into each other before now if you've been living right next door to the shop?"

His response was a sheepish grin. "I only docked there a couple of days ago. My company's doing the rehab on the property."

"For how long?" Tension tightened her shoulders.

"Six, eight months. Why? Is that a problem?"

Yes, it's going to be a little hard to jettison you from my life when you're working three hundred yards from Miami Confidential. She smiled, lying through her teeth. "Of course not."

Chapter Seven

She began backing toward the door. "I'll just go and get your things now."

"My stuff's in the aft quarters."

"And aft means…?"

A smile shone in his dark eyes. "The back. Aft is short for after—as in *after* the rest of the boat has gone by."

"That'll come in handy if I'm ever faced with a parts-of-a-boat quiz."

He grinned just enough to reveal straight, white teeth. "Left-hand drawer as you're facing the bed."

"Got it," she said. "Do I need a key or anything?"

"The dock master has a spare. I'll call him and give him a heads-up."

"I'll be back in about half an hour."

"Thanks." His voice dropped, doing fabulous things to her stomach. "And thanks for the kiss. Powerful medicine. I'm feeling much…stronger."

She left the room, her lips still tingling. Not just her lips, actually. There wasn't a nerve ending in her body that wasn't dancing with residual delight from his kiss.

Julia was so lost in her pleasant musings that it took a second for her brain to process the topic of conversation spilling from behind the partially open door to the nurses' lounge.

"…something to do with that rich lady's kidnapping."

"I agree. I saw the syringe, and I'm telling you, it was atropine," one of them said.

"That's creepy," another said, her voice quivering slightly.

"Johnson was creepy. Donnie, the cute guy who does the three-to-eleven shift, well, he said he saw Johnson arguing with a Latino man yesterday. Said the man was dressed like he was from housekeeping, but he had buffed nails. As soon as Donnie went into the room, the guy with the manicure bolted."

"Maybe he tried to kill Johnson," one of them speculated.

"We'll know in twenty-four hours. If he makes it, he'll be fine. But for the record, I think it was the woman."

What woman? Julia wondered, straining to hear.

"Maybe. She has called a lot."

"But only to check on his progress. She never wanted to talk to Johnson directly. Plus, she didn't seem all that happy when I told her that he would recover."

"I think—"

Julia jumped away from the door the instant she spotted the detectives and three crime scene techs exiting Johnson's room down the hall. They had only a few evidence bags, so she guessed whoever had gone after Johnson was a professional.

She hurried back to her car, dialing Rachel as she jogged through the lot. "We need the phone logs from the second floor nurses' station. I know we've had a tap on his room phone, but someone's been calling the nurses directly for information."

She told her boss all about the mystery woman and the medical staff's speculations about what had been injected into Johnson's heart.

"Did you conclude matters with Mr. Young?"

"Kind of."

"Julia?" Rachel pressed, a note of warning in her voice.

"We're handling his foster sister's wedding, Rachel. And I just learned his company is rehabbing the Costal Marina Yacht Club. It's going to be hard for me to avoid him."

"I don't like it, Julia. Call it intuition, call it whatever you want. Luke Young just seems like trouble to me. He's a smart man. I don't think it will take him long to discover that there's more to Weddings Your Way than just a bridal shop. Botero's security team is suspicious. The Miami PD is suspicious. We don't need another complication at this point."

"He won't be a problem," Julia said with more confidence than she was feeling at the moment. It was her job to ensure that Luke Young *wasn't* a problem.

"The safest course of action is to sever all ties," Rachel advised.

"Trust me, Rachel, I know what I'm doing."

"Do you?"

Yes. No. Julia blew out a frustrated breath as she replayed Rachel's cryptic question on her drive to the marina. It was a quick trip, maybe five minutes. Not nearly enough time to sort out her feelings. Though, Lord knew, they needed intense, remedial sorting.

She stopped at the dock master's hut for the keys. "Hut" was generous; it was more like a shack.

The thatched roof was in dire need of repair and the last hurricane season had taken a toll on the property. The yacht club had been closed for the past decade. It was a modest place by Miami standards—a three-story building with lots of arches, the stucco flaking and crumbling from years of neglect. The adjoining pool wasn't in much better shape, but the place had potential.

The slips were a different story. Row upon row of glistening white boats swayed on the gently rippling tide. Julia parked at the end of dock three, shielding her eyes as she hunted for the slip number the dock master had provided.

Gulls squawked overhead and a pelican flapped to a clumsy landing atop one of the pilings as she traversed the worn planking. The *Freedom* was at the end of the dock, secured to polished cleats by expertly tied ropes.

"I'm impressed," she mumbled as she climbed aboard.

Weddings Your Way had a yacht available for charter. Uncle Carlos had one, as well. Owning a boat in Miami was almost a requirement for residency. As she admired the richly varnished wood railings and the high-tech gadgets, she suffered a pang of envy.

Her father had refused to own a boat. Understandable given the horrible circumstances of their crossing from Cuba. Julia had been too young to make the association of water and death, so she regarded the vessel with admiration.

Ducking her head, she cleared the hatch and descended into the aft cabin. She was welcomed by the ghost of Luke's cologne. Breathing deeply, she savored the scent, then glanced around, envisioning him in these surroundings.

She hadn't expected it to be so...*homey*. The cabin was dominated by a large bed, neatly made, and decorated in nautical blues and whites. It was compact and orderly, but the shelves were littered with personal items. A photograph of Luke and Carmen flanking a large fish. Another one of Luke parasailing. A few items waited to be hung on the paneled walls. One was from a local boys club, an appreciation award for his volunteer efforts. The other was a certificate in recognition of thirty days of sobriety courtesy of the Keller Drug and Alcohol Rehabilitation Clinic. Her stomach plummeted.

Taking it from the ledge, she inspected it more closely and realized it wasn't Luke's. "A.J. Taggert?" The name was familiar. Luke had mentioned it but she couldn't instantly recall if he was an employee or some kid he'd mentored.

Carefully, she replaced it in the exact spot she'd found it, then knelt down to reach for the drawer at the foot of the bed. She had already opened it when she remembered Luke had said the left-hand drawer.

Blatant curiosity got the better of her when she spied a tidy stack of letters secured with a rubber band tucked in the back of the drawer. "None of your business," she chided, to no avail.

Hating herself the entire time, Julia reached in and retrieved nearly a dozen letters. Luke's name and a post office box address were typed on the first plain, white envelope. Using the tip of her nail, Julia lifted the flap and extracted a folded sheet of inexpensive stationary. She half expected to find gushing professions of love from an old girlfriend.

Instead, a chill fell over her as she read aloud the words crafted from cut and pasted newsprint. "You deserve to die and you will. Soon."

LUKE KNEW THE MINUTE A.J. came into his hospital room that he was coming down from a high. So much for sobriety.

A.J., his former foster brother and current thorn in his side, sprawled in one of the chairs, his feet tapping against the floor. "Wow, dude, you got blown up. That sucks."

"What are you doing here?" Luke growled, then raised his hand. "Forget it. You'll just lie to me."

A.J. was emaciated and, thanks to his addiction, looked several years older than twenty-six. His blond hair was a dirty, shaggy mess, and his blue eyes were bloodshot and glassy. "I had a little, um, setback," he said belligerently.

He also sounded sorry; hell, he probably was. Then again, A.J. was always sincere when he needed another fix.

"Nothing has changed, A.J.," Luke said, hating that he was forced to play the bad guy. "I'm not giving you any money. We both know you'll just shoot it into your veins."

A.J. jumped from the chair and began pacing the small confines of the room. He reminded Luke of a skittish, caged animal. But it was a cage he'd built himself. "I didn't come here to hit you up. Honest," A.J. insisted. "I came cause I heard about your accident."

"Really? Who told you?"

A.J. hung his head. "Carmen."

Luke experienced a rush of anger. "I thought we agreed that you'd stay away from her unless you were clean."

"She came to me," he insisted in a childish whine. "She was all freaked out that you wouldn't let her come to see you. Tommy was with her."

Blowing out a breath, Luke felt his anger meld into frustration. As much as he loved Carmen, he didn't think she made the best choices. Especially when it came to their "family." Carmen was the self-appointed peacemaker in the group. Despite what had happened nearly two decades ago, she was determined to include Tommy and Betty in their lives.

Carmen and A.J. had continued to live with Mrs. Anderson after Frank's death. Maybe that was why she still felt such an alliance to them.

Luke wasn't so inclined. Betty Anderson was decent enough, but Luke blamed Tommy for A.J.'s addiction. They were the same age. Tommy had started experimenting with drugs and taken A.J. along for the ride. Only Tommy beat it. A.J. never did. Big time.

If A.J. didn't clean up his act, he'd wind up dead or in jail. Luke had spent the last year trying to keep him clean. It wasn't working. A.J. was into debt with his dealer for almost fifty grand, and if this visit was any indication, he was back on the needle. Not a good sign, since A.J.'s sobriety and his freedom depended on him staying clean long enough to testify against his supplier. Unfortunately, that trial was still months away.

"Tommy was real concerned, too," A.J. continued. "He said you were at your girlfriend's place. The one you almost married."

The hairs on the back of Luke's neck prickled. "She isn't my girlfriend, and how did Tommy know that?"

"From the news," A.J. answered, then sniffed loudly, using his sleeve as a tissue. "The cops are claiming the explosion was a gas leak, but Carmen told us about the kidnapping at that fancy wedding shop. Think your girlfriend was in on it or something?"

Luke scoffed. "No. I spoke to the cops last night and it *was* a gas leak."

"Man, you coulda been blown to bits or something."

"I wasn't," Luke replied, checking his watch. Julia should have been back by now. "Who'd you con into paying for your fix, Carmen or Tommy?"

"It wasn't like that," A.J. insisted. "Carmen gave me a few dollars 'cause I'm a little behind on the rent. Tommy tossed me a few bucks for groceries."

"I'll have a talk with them."

"You can't do that," A.J. pleaded, moving to the bedside. "You know how it is, Luke. You go through rehab, your friends and family are proud of you. You fall off the wagon and everyone bails. I came here to ask for help. I know I screwed up and I want to go back to Keller. Get back on track. It was just this one time, I swear."

Luke heard the desperate plea in his foster brother's voice, and even though he was supposed to practice "tough love," it was easier said than done. "I'll see what I can do. It isn't a hotel, A.J. The place has a waiting list." Luke rubbed his hands over his face and sighed heavily. "How much do you owe your landlord?"

"Just a hundred," A.J. swore. "I got fired from the fish place last week so I came up a little short on the rent."

"I'll catch you up, but you're going to work it off."

"Thanks. There's an ATM around the corn—"

"No cash," Luke interrupted, his tone absolute. "I'll pay the landlord directly. I'll have groceries delivered to your place by tonight. I want you at the job site by 7:00 a.m. You're running out of second chances."

A.J. immediately seemed relieved and all of about twelve years old when he grabbed Luke's hand and gave it a squeeze. "Thanks, man, really. I won't mess up this time. I promise."

Luke was again put in the "bad guy" role, when all he wanted was to keep A.J. safe and sober. "Stay away from Tommy."

"He's an okay guy," A.J. protested.

"He's an addict."

"Not anymore," A.J. said, admiration beaming from his diluted blue eyes.

"Tommy may not be using anymore, but he's still an addict."

"You should cut him some slack," A.J. suggested. "I think you're just weird around him because you killed his old man and you feel guilty. Carmen likes him."

"Carmen likes everyone," Luke countered.

He wondered if A.J. was right. Did he have some sort of suppressed guilt? He shook his head. Luke had made his peace with the family from prison. Betty Anderson, Frank's widow, had forgiven him, even going so far as to visit him regularly.

"Don't worry about me. Focus on yourself, A.J."

"I will, I mean I am." A.J.'s fingers drummed against the chair arms. "So, what's up with you and this girl?"

Luke's mind instantly conjured the memory of having Julia in his arms. The sweet taste of her mouth, the soft, silken feel of her hair slipping through his fingers. "Nothing, so far."

A.J.'s dim eyes brightened. "Tommy said she was really hot."

"How would he know?"

"Saw her on the news. So, you gonna try to hook up with her?"

"Maybe."

"Sa-weet."

"You might want to think about improving your vocabulary," Luke joked before checking his watch again. Where was Julia? Given the gunfire and the explosion, he was understandably worried. The woman seemed to trip over disaster on a regular basis.

"Thanks for squaring things with my landlord, and I promise I'll be at your place by seven sharp. Thanks, man. And try to stay out of trouble."

Luke was surprised into laughing. "Try taking your own advice. I'll talk to a few people and see how soon I can get you back into Keller. Until then, I want your skinny butt at NA meetings every day."

A.J.'s head bobbed like one of those nodding dolls they gave away on fan nights at the ballpark. "I'm so there, Luke. Swear."

"Tell Carmen to stop worrying about me. She's got enough on her plate with the wedding next weekend."

"Got it. Anything I can do for you?"

"Stay clean," Luke reiterated firmly.

A.J. left, and as always, Luke wondered if it might be the last time he'd see him breathing.

His concern for Julia was growing, but he didn't have a phone number for her. But he guessed Carmen would. Leaning over to the night table, he grabbed up the receiver and started pressing buttons.

THE NOTES ALL THREATENED Luke's life and raised an important question in Julia's mind. Why?

Why would someone want to kill him? Why hadn't he turned them over to the police after the shooting? "Why didn't—"

Her cell phone vibrated. "Garcia."

"Where are you?" Rachel demanded.

"Getting clothes for Luke."

"You need to come to the office. Now."

"Is it Sonya?"

"No. It's you."

That didn't sound good. Placing the letters on the end of the bed, she opened the correct drawer and grabbed a pair of jeans and a T-shirt for Luke. Pressing her lips together, she weighed her options. It wasn't a tough decision, so she grabbed up the envelopes and hurriedly left the boat.

She didn't stop at the dock master's office to return the keys. At this point, she didn't know how, where or when she'd be returning the threatening letters. Only that it wouldn't happen until she figured out why someone was intent on killing Luke.

Rachel and the entire team were assembled in the conference room. Julia felt all eyes turn in her direction when she entered.

Rachel was at the head of the table. Seated next to her was Sophie Brooks. Sophie was a tall, willowy blonde who fronted as the invitation designer for Weddings Your Way. She was former CIA, leaving New York City in order to work for Miami Confidential. She was pretty secretive about her past, so Julia knew only two things about the woman: 1) she avoided men and 2) she refused to give up her love for panty hose, even in a city as hot as Miami.

Rafe Montoya was in the next seat. Of all the Miami Confidential agents, Julia was probably closest to him. They shared similar pasts. Rafe came from humble Latin roots and he'd done time as a DEA agent.

Clare Myers sat opposite him. She was a tiny woman who'd traded in her job as an IRS auditor to work as Miami Confidential's accountant. She was a math whiz and could follow a paper trail better than anyone Julia knew.

Nicole O'Shae was next to Clare. They were on opposite ends of the style spectrum. Nicole was the Weddings Your Way photographer and had an eye for detail. Her grasp of visual minutia was amazing. She wore her jet-black hair in pigtails and sported some kind of yin-yang tattoo on the back of her neck. She had at least a dozen piercings and a passion for vintage gothic clothing.

Samantha Peters was the thin, quiet one. Julia always felt a little uncomfortable around Samantha. Not because she wasn't friendly; she was. It had to do with Samantha's past. She'd spent years as an FBI profiler, so Julia always felt as if she had to measure every word she spoke around her. Though Samantha had softened a little. A lot, actually. Thanks to Alex Graham. The two had met when his sister was hit by the limo that kidnapped Sonya. The sister had recovered, but Samantha was never the same since falling in love.

Isabelle Rush, the strawberry blonde with the light brown eyes, sat sipping some juice. Isabelle had been a legend at the DEA. Every woman who came after her was held to the "Isabelle standard." The bar was quite high.

Jeff Walsh was leaning back in his chair, his fingers laced behind his head. His front as the music coordinator at Weddings Your Way hid an impressive past with the Dallas PD. He was tall and muscular, with brown hair, light green eyes and that kind of bad-boy appeal that had women flocking to him.

Julia moved toward the vacant seat normally occupied by Ethan Whitehawk. He fronted as the on-site handyman, when in fact he was a master at investigation. As she pulled out her seat, she wondered why Ethan wasn't at the meeting.

Julia felt tense as she scooted her chair close to the table, the letters still clutched in her hands. "What's up?"

"We have confirmation from the lab that C-4 was used at your place last night."

Julia digested the information. "The explosive of choice for the Laderan drug cartel."

"And Esterhaus," Rachel said, passing out copies to all the members of the team. "He's in prison, but the feds believe he's calling the shots from the inside."

Julia felt her heart sink into her toes. "So we're now thinking Esterhaus was behind the shooting, and the blowing up of my apartment?"

"Too soon to be certain," Rachel said. "But it's definitely a possibility."

Samantha cleared her throat, then said, "Except that Esterhaus never knew about Julia's involvement in his arrest and conviction. If this was some sort of revenge or vendetta, the more logical target would be Luke Young."

Jeff shook his head. "But she and Young

weren't together until yesterday afternoon. How would Esterhaus or his people put all that together in enough time to rig explosives at her apartment? I don't think the two things are related."

"Me, either," Rafe agreed. "The shooting might be Esterhaus, but the C-4 at your apartment is vintage Laderan cartel. Given that the limo driver had a Laderan phone number, I think it's a pretty safe bet to assume they're behind Sonya's kidnapping. I'd also bet good money that they're the ones who tried to kill him at the hospital. He must know something."

"Which we can't explore until and if he regains consciousness," Rachel said. "Julia, you said you thought you saw someone dressed like a doctor leaving the floor just before Johnson was attacked?"

She nodded. "No look at his face. We should get our hands on the hospital security tapes. Maybe we'll get lucky."

Rachel agreed, assigning the task to Rafe. "I've sent Ethan to Ladera. We need intel on the drug cartel and Juan DeLeon."

"Juan can't be involved with them," Julia insisted. "If Sonya trusts him, then we should, too."

"I've been all over Juan DeLeon," Isabelle said. "The guy is squeaky clean. A bit of a do-gooder, but nothing to indicate he's ever been involved with the cartel. The only marginally questionable thing I've found is an ex-wife named Maggie who fried her brain on drugs. From all accounts, she hid her drug problem from Juan. He only found out after she suffered her psychotic break. She's in a sanatorium in Ladera. Ethan is going to see her while he's down there."

"I may have proof that Esterhaus was behind the shooting," Julia said, carefully sliding the envelopes into plain view of her colleagues. "I found these on Luke's boat."

Everyone but Rachel leaned in for a closer look as she used a pencil to open the folded sheet. "I didn't know what they were, so my prints are on them."

"We'll run them through forensics," Rachel announced.

"That, um, could be a problem," Julia said. "I need to put them back or he might get suspicious."

"Not a prob. We can keep the originals. Give me thirty minutes with Sophie's help and I'll make replicas," Nicole chirped. "I can scan them and doctor up the scans so he'll never know the difference."

"Good, get on it," Rachel directed. "Rafe, see what you can find out about any associates Esterhaus may have hired here in Miami. Jeff, you stick close to Luke and—"

"He'll spot a shadow inside an hour," Julia argued. "Luke is naturally distrustful. If Jeff—or anyone else—tries to insinuate themselves into his life right now, he'll know it. Let me handle Luke."

Rachel was shaking her head. "You're out, Julia. We're going to send you to a different location until we get this sorted though. I'm not willing to risk your safety."

"Out? Are you kidding me? I'm not hanging Luke out to dry a second time. And," she began, ticking things off on her fingers, "Sonya is my best friend. Carlos is still in the hospital. There's the Lopez wedding preparations. It isn't like I can just drop off the face of the earth. I refuse to be banished to another office while you guys hunt for her kidnappers, leaving Luke to…well to—" Julia's mouth snapped shut when she saw the startled faces of her coworkers.

"Done getting all that out of your system?" Rachel asked, her gaze level and unyielding.

"I said a different location, not another office."

Julia felt her mouth dry to dust as anger simmered in the pit of her stomach. This was it? She was getting fired in front of everyone? Pounding her palms on the table, she waited for the sound to stop reverberating through the room before she spoke. "I owe Luke. If Esterhaus is after him, it's my fault, and I have a duty and a responsibility to make sure nothing happens to him." She felt her stomach churn at the thought, but dismissed the confused feelings that had haunted her since Luke had walked back into her life. Now wasn't the time nor the place to address them. "Isn't that at the heart of what we do here? Protect innocent people? I know you hold Luke's past over—"

Rachel's raised hand silenced her. "You're out of the Botero kidnapping," she clarified. "Your new assignment is to protect Luke Young."

Chapter Eight

"Where are you?" Luke demanded in her ear. He sounded...frustrated? Worried? Annoyed?

Julia balanced the cell phone between her ear and her shoulder so she could shift the Jeep into fourth. "Driving," she answered placatingly.

"You should have been here fifteen minutes ago. I've been going nuts."

"So shoot me. No, wait, someone already tried that."

"Not funny," Luke warned. "The doc was just here. Apparently there's a problem on the floor, so they're short-staffed. Sounds like it'll take about an hour and a half for them to release me from the hospital."

A little more than a problem. An attempted murder, but she didn't think it wise to pass that along. Julia checked the dash clock.

"Good. Then I can run a couple of errands before I swing by the hospital"

"I need clothes," he reminded her.

"I've got yours, but I need some, too. Everything I own was incinerated in the…gas explosion. I need to run to the store to buy some basics." *And give the team time to dummy-up realistic copies of the notes, then put them back in place.*

"Damn, sorry. I wasn't thinking. Of course you do. I can take a cab if—"

"Don't be silly," Julia exclaimed. "I'll be there before noon. By the way, how did you get my cell number?"

"Carmen," he admitted, genuine affection in his tone.

"Right."

As soon as she hung up, Julia made a quick U-turn and doubled back to the row of trendy boutiques off Biscayne Boulevard. She parked and unlocked the glove box. Shoving her SIG-Sauer to one side, she felt around for her wallet. She smiled sadly as she relocked the compartment. Sonya often criticized her failing to embrace the concept of carrying a purse. Of course, Sonya had no way of knowing that Julia's choice was more a function of practicality than bucking cultural norms. It was hard to chase down the bad guys with ten pounds of junk dangling from your shoulder.

After tucking her wallet in her pocket, she made a mental list of the things she'd need. Reaching for the polished chrome handle on the heavy door of the boutique, she recalled the last time she'd been here.

It was right after Sonya and Juan's engagement. That had been eighteen months ago, one of those perfect girlfriend days, marked by overspending and lots of laughter. She swallowed a lump in her throat, wondering what Sonya was doing right now. *Somewhere Deep in the Jungle…*

SONYA STUMBLED when her sandaled foot caught beneath one of the vines snaking across the path. Path, she thought, was charitable at best. It was little more than a narrow passageway through thick, dense foliage.

"Keep moving," one of her captors said in Spanish. He punctuated the remark by using the butt of his rifle to jab her in the back.

The breath whooshed from her lungs at the unexpected impact, and tears welled in her eyes. A smart retort died on her tongue. In the days—weeks—since the kidnapping she'd learned a few basic rules of survival. Holding her tongue was one of them.

Particularly with this one. Her captors all looked the same. They wore full fatigues and scuffed military boots. All she could see was their eyes, the remainder of their faces concealed by the filthy bandannas they always donned in her presence. The men worked in details of two or three at any given time. This morning she was with the Bad Ones.

The leader was a beefy, muscular guy who seemed to intimidate his comrades almost as much as he scared her. It wasn't so much what he said as the pitiless blackness of his eyes. They were hard and dark and full of menace. From her brief time with him, Sonya knew he enjoyed inflicting pain.

Perspiration trickled down her back as she trudged forward, ferns and branches slapping at her arms, face and neck. Insects buzzed all around, humming in her ears. The air was thick with humidity. It surprised her to realize she was growing used to the stench of rotting vegetation.

Mist swirled in the air as they marched her closer to the thunderous rumbling waterfall deep in the jungle. Standing beneath the cold mountain water rushing off the edge of the cliff was the best part of her day. It allowed her to remove the top layer of grime from her itchy, bug-bitten skin.

She mopped her brow with the sleeve of the olive-drab T-shirt they'd made her wear since they'd forced her at gunpoint to disembark from the twin-engine plane. Salt from perspiration stung the cut on her thumb. Her throat clogged with a mishmash of raw emotion. The memory of the knife blade slicing through her skin was fresh in her mind. The pain had filled her entire consciousness. And while it probably was little more than a paper cut, she'd felt violated. Nobody had ever hurt her physically in her life, and the fact that these men could and would terrified her right to her core.

Panic, anger and frustration clashed in her chest, causing her to squeeze her eyes closed so she wouldn't cry. She didn't give a damn if they saw her weep, but she knew once she started, she might never stop. She bit her lip hard and kept on walking.

Juan and her father must be frantic by now. She didn't want to think of what it might have done to them to get a note that included her bloody fingerprint. But she had to hold on. Either or both of them would find their way to her. She clung to that thread of hope as she staggered through the thick underbrush.

To maintain her sanity, she summoned happy memories of Juan and her father. Of lazy afternoons on the beach. Of holidays and pleasant parties. Anything to keep her focused. She had to survive.

The man with the dead eyes roughly grabbed her by the shoulder, spinning her around as he clicked open his switchblade. The sharp knife glinted in the sunlight splintering through the canopy of trees overhead.

With a single flick, he sliced the twine binding her wrists. Automatically, Sonya rubbed the sore, raw welts where the rope had burned her skin. One of the underlings handed her a threadbare cloth and a small square of soap, then gestured with his head that it was time for her daily dousing.

She knew her humiliation was important to her captors. Thrusting her chin out proudly, she again refused his command to strip. There was no way she'd let any of these thugs see her naked.

With her spine royally stiff, she marched toward the waterfall. Sonya waited until she reached the mossy boulders at the water's edge before shuffling out of her jute sandals. A tiny sound rumbled in her throat when she spotted the small red-and-black snake slithering a few feet ahead of her into the water.

Even fully clothed as she was, the frigid water came as a shock. It was a good fifty degrees cooler than the air temperature. The lye soap felt slimy as she tried in vain to work up a lather. It was a far cry from the sweet smelling, hand-milled soaps she was accustomed to, but it got the job done. She was able to tolerate the freezing water for about five minutes before her fingers numbed.

The ill-fitting T-shirt clung to her as she stepped out from under the water, teeth chattering. Ignoring the muffled taunts from her captors, she squeezed excess water from the ends of her dark hair.

"Time's up, *bruja*." Dead Eye Guy was the only one who ever spoke to her in English. Educated English at that. It was one of the things that set him apart from the other kidnappers, rebels or whatever they were.

One of the other issues she'd had way too much time to ponder was why? If this was about money, collecting a ransom from her father, why fly her to this godforsaken jungle? Miami had warehouses, industrial complexes, shipyards, any number of other places to stash her away until the payoff, which she knew her father would hand over.

Sonya wiggled her damp feet into the rough, scratchy sandals and returned to the edge of the jungle where her captors waited, automatic weapons slung over their shoulders. Defiantly, she held out her arms, fists balled, while new twine was twisted around her wrists.

She tilted her chin, looking the leader in the eye. He backhanded her, sending her flying facefirst into the spongy dirt.

Sonya's cheek stung as she stumbled to regain her footing. The men mocked her, likening her to the pigs they kept penned back at the compound. There was a brief discussion among them about whether or not they should dip her into the frigid river again to teach her a lesson, until one of them mentioned their patron.

It wasn't the first time they'd referred to this mysterious person, who was obviously calling the shots from a safe distance. Her instincts told her it had something to do with Juan's politics. Ladera was in the midst of elections, and her beloved Juan was doing everything in his power to restore Ladera to its pre-drug-exportation days. His strong convictions and policies were just two of the many things she adored about him.

She should be home, planning their wedding. Not trudging through some vile jungle with a band of rifle-toting goons. Her poor father. Surely he was beside himself with worry.

Guilt mingled with her frustration and anger. She felt the depth of her father's un-conditional love even here in this hell.

Sonya prayed for strength, for patience and mostly for rescue as she was marched back to the camp. Her captors were careful to keep her on the path. Occasionally a plane would pass overhead, and she guessed they didn't want to risk being spotted.

The smell from the half-dozen pigs in their makeshift pen wafted to her nostrils. Sonya's hut was farther into the forest, but she could still hear and smell the pigs. It was a wood-and-metal structure, complete with a dirt floor and a full complement of creepy-crawly things.

She was shoved inside, hands still bound so she couldn't brace herself. She fell to the dirt floor. The door closed, blocking out the light. She heard the heavy chain being wrapped around the handles. Her resolve crumbled. Curling into a fetal position, she gave in and sobbed—then jerked upright abruptly at the sound of a single gunshot.

"HOW ARE YOU?" Carmen's voice on the phone conveyed her worry.

"I'm fine," Luke declared, hoping to allay her fears. He tried to fold the thin hospital pillow into a more comfortable backrest, holding the phone between chin and shoulder. "I have a very hard head."

"I already know that. Luke," Carmen added in a barely audible whisper. "Don't be mad at me, okay?"

"Why would I be mad? And why are we whispering?" he whispered.

"Dalton is in the other room."

Luke frowned. "He doesn't give you phone privileges?"

"Of course he does," Carmen insisted, clearly irritated by the jab. "I just don't want to upset him. We need to talk. I'll pick you up."

Two quick knocks on the door prevented Luke from giving an immediate answer. Julia stood in the doorway, a bag in one hand and her keys in the other. "Sorry," she mouthed, starting to retreat when she saw he was on the phone. He waved her into the room. "Upset him how?" Luke asked, winking at Julia.

"I'd rather do this in person. Can I just come over there? Now?"

Luke reluctantly dragged his eyes off Julia's amazing, exotic features and gave his full attention to Carmen. "Do what in person? What's wrong?"

"I'll tell you when I see you. That's what 'in person' means. I can be at the hospital in less than an hour. Can you wait that long?"

"I already have a ride," he said, unapologetic as his gaze roamed appreciatively over Julia. She'd been shot at, blown up and sleep deprived, yet she still managed to look sexy as hell. He was particularly fond of the strappy, layered T-shirts she favored. Especially since they fell about an inch shy of the waistband of her pants. That little hint of flat, bronzed belly caused a stir in his nether regions.

At Carmen's long silence he said, "I'll be at the boat in about an hour. I've got a meeting at three. I can probably reschedule that if you need me to."

He heard her expel a breath. "I've got to meet Mrs. Mitchell this afternoon. She wants to review the seating chart for the hundredth time. My future mother-in-law is very *detail* oriented," Carmen quipped with a resigned little laugh. "With the wedding so close, she's in full freak-out mode."

"About what?" Luke asked.

"Nothing and everything," Carmen insisted. "Are you still coming for dinner on Monday?"

He grimaced, but said, "Wouldn't miss it for the world."

"Good, I want everyone to be comfortable. Dalton has a meeting, but he'll join us after dinner. I really want you to get to know him better. In seven days, we'll all be family."

Gee, great, he thought unenthusiastically. "That's what you've always wanted."

"You have, too, only you won't do anything about it. Or, wait!" Her tone grew louder and more excited. "Is your ride that woman? Not her," Carmen said flatly. "Geez, Luke, she's nice and a great seamstress, but I think she's a flake.

"If I'd have known she was *that* Julia, I wouldn't have sent you within a mile of her. I most definitely wouldn't have given you her phone number. Wasn't it punishment enough that she left you standing at the altar? And your reunion hasn't gone too smoothly. She's got her own personal black cloud, and I don't want you caught up in her next disaster."

He smiled at his sister's concerns but didn't take them to heart. She was, after all, about to marry Dalton the Dweeb, which hardly made her an expert on interpersonal relationships. "My ride's waiting and I still have to throw on some clothes. Want me to call you back when I get to the boat?"

"No," she said in a huff. "I'll come by after my thing with Mrs. Mitchell."

He placed the phone on its cradle, then cocked his head to one side to admire Julia openly. She was at the window, her long, tapered fingers separating the blinds as she peered outside.

The fact that she was distracted worked in his favor. It allowed his eyes to linger on the full, rounded slope of her derriere. His gaze moved higher, and he almost groaned when he saw the dimples, those cute little indentations at her lower back that made his fingers tingle with the desire to touch. If he kept this up, his jeans wouldn't fit.

The rustling sound of him tossing off the

sheet got Julia's attention. She turned and watched him swing his toned, muscular legs to the floor. Her mouth opened, then snapped shut. Seeing him standing there in his boxers sealed her throat.

Mutely, she thrust the bag in his general direction, stiffening her arm to keep as much distance between them as possible. It was definitely an exercise in self-preservation. Seeing him nearly naked was almost more than her frazzled, needy libido could handle.

His torso was buff, sculpted. Broad shoulders tapered down to a trim waist. Then fabric, then those great legs. If he had a physical flaw, she sure couldn't find it.

That was troublesome, but not as bad as trying to tell herself she didn't care about this man. For six years, she'd been sure her memories of Luke were tainted by revisionist history. No man could be this perfect. He was smart, gorgeous, funny and about a million other things that she found appealing.

Over time, she'd convinced herself that her remembrances were all blown out of proportion. Particularly when she'd measured and dismissed every man who came into her life based on that extremely short, long-ago encounter with Luke. Other men paled badly in comparison. Now, being with him again, she began to question herself. What if she hadn't fantasized the real Luke? What if he was "the one"?

She recalled the way her father had spoken of the first time he'd met her mother. He'd often said that he knew he wanted to marry her about an hour into their first date.

Was it genetic? Or was this attraction to Luke simply lust masquerading as real feelings? Not that it mattered. It wasn't like she was free to welcome him into her crazy life. Doing so would mean having to tell him all her secrets, and that was impossible. For a whole raft of reasons, not the least of which was getting fired.

Being shot at was starting to look like the easy part of her week. Luke took the bag. The tips of their fingers brushed together, sending wave after wave of sexually inspired zings through her nervous system. She peered up into his dark, smoldering eyes and prayed her knees wouldn't buckle. "S-shouldn't you get dressed?"

"Yeah," he said, though he didn't move an inch.

Heat from his body intensified as the air

between them crackled and sizzled. The glint in his gaze was powerful, silently conveying both curiosity and passion. It was a pretty heady experience to see all the things she was feeling mirrored in his eyes.

And dangerous. Julia needed to get herself back on track. She didn't want to risk letting her desires get in the way of her job. A job she couldn't do if her judgment was continually clouded by lust.

As he strode toward the bathroom to dress, she watched the tight, toned outline of his butt. So much for keeping her hormones in check.

While Luke put on the jeans and shirt she'd gotten from his boat, Julia received a text message that the team had put the dummied-up notes back in the drawer. Now she just had to find a way to stick close to him without arousing his suspicions.

She grimaced. *Arousing* was a very poor word choice, since she was—very. *Just like Vegas,* she thought grimly. It wasn't as if she was sex starved or anything. She liked Luke. A lot. A whole lot.

Too much.

She had to think of him as an assignment, period. Find out who was threatening him and fix it. Nothing else. That resolve lasted until he stepped from the bathroom, running his fingers through his mussed, dark hair. He winced. "Ouch."

"How's your head?" she asked.

"Fine, except for the glue stuck in my hair. Ready?"

You have no idea. "Sure."

Julia was the envy of more than just a few of the female nurses as she exited the hospital with Luke. She grabbed the sunglasses she'd hooked on the front of her shirt, and pointed in the direction of her Jeep.

"I'm starving," he said after they were in the car. "Any chance you'd join me for lunch before we swing by your place for my car?"

"I'll do you one better," she replied, easing out into the traffic. "Do you like arroz con pollo?"

"Not when I try to make it."

"When I prepare it, it's a thing of beauty."

"So are you."

She smiled. "Thank you. Can we get back to discussing your need for nourishment?"

"In a minute," he replied, reaching over to close one hand on her knee. "Are we headed somewhere?"

"The parking lot of what used to be my apartment."

His fingers tightened on her leg. "Thanks for the GPS update, but you know that wasn't what I meant."

"I can't answer that kind of question."

"I need you to." Absently, he started making maddening little circles with the pad of his thumb. "I don't want to get jerked around again."

She stiffened slightly, then defensively said, "I don't recall jerking you around. I didn't introduce you to Esterhaus. You did that all by yourself."

"Not that," he clarified in an even, measured tone. "I was talking about after. When the dust settled and you disappeared on me."

I couldn't face you. I felt guilty. Guilty for involving you in the case, guilty for duping you into almost marrying me, and extremely confused by feelings for you I had no business having. "Luke, what was supposed to happen? I thought we both agreed a day or so ago that our whirlwind romance was a mistake."

"The rushing into a wedding part, yes. But I don't understand why you evaporated off the face of the earth. You left your waitressing job. Your apartment was empty. I know, because I went every place I could think of trying to find you."

"I've apologized, Luke. What do you want from me?"

"A chance."

"At what?"

"I don't know," he snapped as he pulled his hand away. "For nature to take its course."

"We set our own courses."

"Thanks for the ride, and it was great seeing you again. I especially liked sharing gunfire and the explosions with you. One thing's for sure, Julia, life is never dull around you. I'll pass on the chicken, though I do appreciate the offer. Just drop me at my car."

"Don't you think you're overreacting a little?" she asked mildly.

His jaw clenched. "I'm not overreacting at all."

It would be impossible to protect him if he blew her off. "What is it with you and your need for instant commitment?"

"I like to know where I stand with people, Julia. Maybe it's because I got passed around as a kid. I learned a long time ago that life's a lot easier when everyone's on the same page."

Her heart squeezed in her chest as the image of a frightened, unwanted little boy flashed in her mind.

"I didn't have a Carlos Botero," he reminded her. "How is he, by the way?"

Finally, a safe topic. "He'll need some rehab, but he sounded better when I called him earlier."

"Any news about his daughter?"

"There's been a ran—" She clamped her mouth shut, wondering how she could make such a stupid, irresponsible mistake.

"A ransom?"

She shot him a quick, panicked glance. "You can't say anything. It could get Sonya killed. Promise me, Luke."

"I would never do anything like that. You'd be amazed to know how well I can keep a secret."

Can't hold a candle to me, pal. "Thanks. I wasn't insinuating that you'd put Sonya at risk, I just, well, I don't want to be the one responsible for any leaks."

"Not a problem."

"Neither is lunch," she said as they neared the turn into the rubble-littered parking area adjacent to her building. "I'd like to cook for you. Surely we can share a meal without mapping out our whole lives, right?"

"Sure," he sighed.

Luke's dark SUV was in the parking lot adjacent to the apartment complex. It was covered in a layer of cement dust, but luckily, hadn't been damaged. Her building was another story. Julia shivered as she slowly drove through the lot, taking in the devastation left in the wake of the bomb. She shuddered, thinking what could have happened if they'd been a foot or so closer when it blew.

"You are *seriously* homeless," Luke remarked. "I can't believe no one was hurt."

"You were."

"Hardly," he said, casting her a sidelong look. "Why doesn't anyone believe me?"

"Um, because your head is glued together?"

"A preexisting condition. It already feels itchy. I'm a fast healer."

"Go back to the boat," she said, nudging his shoulder. "It'll only take me a minute or two at the market, then I'll be right behind you." *So will Jeff Walsh,* she added silently.

Luke started to get out of the Jeep, then stopped and turned to her. Slowly, he lifted his hand to her face, gently tracing the tip of his finger along her jawline.

The action caused a little shiver to trickle down her neck. Heat built in her stomach as he bent forward, his mouth a mere whisper from hers. Julia's knuckles turned white as she gripped the steering wheel for dear life. She was pretty sure that if she allowed herself to touch him, she wouldn't be able to stop.

His minty breath washed over her face, but he didn't kiss her. Several achingly long seconds passed, and when she couldn't stand it any longer, she closed the distance between them by pressing her lips to his.

It took another second for her to process that he wasn't responding.

Nothing. Nada. Zippo.

Some carnal part of her took hold. Taking her hands off the wheel, she grabbed fistfuls of his shirt and practically yanked him across the console. Her tongue flicked out, teasing the seam of his lips.

Still nothing.

Uncurling her fingers, she flattened her palms against his body, exhilarated and mildly amused when she felt the rapid pounding of his heart. Luke was not as immune as he pretended. Okay, he wanted to play games? She'd play.

She gently drew his lower lip between her teeth and then used her tongue to toy with it as her hands moved up, exploring the contours of his chest and shoulders. She feathered him with tiny kisses as her fingers twined through his thick hair until the tips met behind his neck.

He sucked in a ragged breath, cupped her face and gently extracted himself from her hold. Passion shone in his dark eyes, but the smile he offered was smug.

She grinned right back at him. "Giving up so soon?"

He kissed her forehead. "I'm not giving up, Julia. I'm just getting started."

Chapter Nine

"That kiss got me seriously hot and bothered."

Julia didn't look in the direction of the familiar male voice. She didn't have to, nor could she. If Luke was watching her unload the groceries, he'd notice if she so much as glanced in Jeff's direction.

"You know what you can do with your hot and bothered, don't you?" she countered sweetly, head lowered.

"Have one hell of a great dream."

"Go away now," she told him. "I've got things under control."

"I'll say," Jeff teased. "If you call melting the guy's shorts under control."

"You're crass and you're annoying me. I don't understand how you get women to date you."

"I give good—"

"Do *not* finish that sentence."

"Backrubs," he said with a chuckle. "Give me a call when you need me to sit on this guy again. Later."

Julia shifted both bags to one hand as she headed down the dock. The sun was warm against her back, the breeze lifting her hair off her neck. Water lapping against the hulls of the moored boats made a tranquil, hypnotic sound. Exactly what she needed to relieve the tension left in the wake of the last kiss she'd shared with Luke.

Rerunning Jeff's comments in her mind brought a wry smile to her lips. She was playing with fire. Again. Only this time she was older and wiser and more aware of the reality of her own feelings. Even if she was trying desperately to deny them. Hell's bells, it wasn't as if she could saunter up to him and say, "The last time we were together, I wasn't allowed to fall for you because I was setting you up for the DEA." Or, "I'm falling for you again but the timing is all wrong because I'm a secret operative for Miami Confidential and I'm here to protect you."

But if she wasn't…

Julia dismissed the thoughts as futile. She had a job to do, and involving her emotions could get Luke killed. Because of the threatening notes, she had to stay close to him. Feigning an interest in him was the most expedient way to accomplish that goal.

Only it wasn't easy and she sure wasn't feigning. Luke Young made her blood sing.

God, this was complicated.

"What took you so long? Chicken put up a fight when you had to kill it yourself?"

"Uh, what?"

Luke reached down and took the bags, then offered her a hand up on deck. "You were frowning."

He released her arm, retrieved the groceries and led her to the well-appointed, if compact, galley. She smelled shampoo and a hint of his cologne as she started to unpack the items she'd grabbed from the store. The smell was stronger than it had been a couple of hours ago, indicating he'd showered while she'd been shopping. The thought of Luke naked and wet had her pulse going into overdrive.

He moved out of her way as she started unloading the grocery bags. "Need help?"

"I always cook alone. Step away from the chicken."

Luke shrugged, then went to sit at the U-shaped table a few feet away. He wasn't sitting so much as lounging. A continuous bench wrapped around the table, creating an upholstered area that he used like a chaise, one leg drawn up. Before long he was tapping his thumb to the beat of the music playing softly in the background.

"Josh Grobin?" she asked. "I wouldn't have pegged you as a torch song fan."

He sent her a sexy smile. "I'm a regular Renaissance man."

She turned and challenged him with her eyes.

"Okay, so Carmen left it here. I thought you might like it." He grabbed a small remote control from the table and suddenly Bruce Springsteen was belting out "Born in the USA." "No one sings like the Boss."

Silently agreeing, she lined up all of her ingredients. Then started opening scaled down drawers and cabinets until she found knives, a cutting board and the deepest pan available. "I've never cooked on a boat before," she said, peeling an onion.

She felt his gaze on her as he asked, "So how did you learn to cook?"

"Necessity." She ignored the stab of nostalgia she felt as she elaborated, "My dad tried, but after an eighteen hour day cutting grass and clipping palm fronds, the best he could manage was opening a can."

"I like food too much to be dependent on cans," Luke remarked. "So if you didn't learn at home, who was your teacher?"

She smiled, drawn into memory. "Mrs. Guerra, the woman who also taught me to sew. Everything on her table was made by hand. Much of it grown in the garden in her backyard."

"She sounds nice," Luke commented, getting up to grab a bottle of water from the small refrigerator. He set one on the counter for her as well.

"She was wonderful," Julia said as she minced garlic. "She was really short. What I remember most, though, is her hands. She had pudgy, stubby fingers, but they were powerful little suckers. She could snap beef bones like they were twigs."

"Sounds real attractive."

Julia scrunched her nose, realizing she wasn't doing a very good job describing the kindly old woman. "She could cook and sew and play the guitar. I remember thinking there was nothing she couldn't do. One minute she'd be making flan, then turn around and start plastering a wall."

"Now you're speaking my language. I like a woman who knows her way around a trowel."

"It's a gift," she agreed, adjusting the temperature on the burner.

"What happened to her?"

"She died about the time I went to Vegas." Julia sucked in a breath and let it out slowly. What she couldn't tell him was that she'd missed the funeral because of the Esterhaus investigation. Not his fault. "Okay, your turn."

From her vantage point, she saw him shrug. His entire body tensed, and it was like watching a curtain fall. The easy, handsome smile was gone, replaced by a hard, granite mask. She shivered at the unexpected look into his psyche. She had wanted truth and she had a feeling she was about to get it.

"Hard to tell one foster home from another. They all sort of run together."

"C'mon," she prodded, determined to get to the bottom of what made Luke tick. "I'm sure if you try, you can think up one positive thing."

"Carmen," he said without hesitation. His features softened. "She made me want to do better. To be better."

"How?"

"She needed me," he said simply. "Needed someone at her back."

"Why?" With the chicken browned, Julia stirred in the rice and other ingredients, then picked up her bottle of water.

Other than the gentle sway of the galley lamp, she had almost forgotten she wasn't on dry land. Leaning her hip against the counter, she turned to look at him. And again she was struck by just how handsome he was. Not pretty handsome—rugged handsome, attractive with just the hint of an edge.

"You're never really part of the family," he explained, running one neatly trimmed nail around the edge of the label that was peeling off the water bottle. "Not unless you get really lucky."

She heard the undertones, and her heart melted. Yes, she had a job to do, but she was also curious about his history. "Since I already know how things worked out for you, what happened to Carmen after…after…"

"She stayed," he said with a humorless little laugh. "The state of Florida felt it was best for her and my foster brother A.J. to stay with Mrs. Anderson and Tommy."

"Did you have his back, too?" Somehow

she knew that he would do whatever he had to do for those he loved. It made her scared and warm at the same time.

"When I could," Luke said, his tone laced with regret. "After I was arrested, A.J. and Tommy got tight, which was a bad mistake."

"Because?"

"Tommy is a chip off the old block. He hides it better, but he's just as toxic and angry as his old man was. But he and A.J. are the same age. You know how that works."

"Yes," she agreed, tipping the bottle to her mouth and swallowing. "Sonya and I have birthdays a week apart." She felt a renewed pang of concern for her missing friend. "Same age, same clothes, same crushes, same crises."

"I wish those were the kinds of things Tommy and A.J. shared."

"Drinking? Drugs?"

He nodded. "Toss in some breaking and entering, shoplifting and other petty crimes, and I think you get the picture."

Ah. "Where was Mrs. Anderson during all this?"

"Selectively ignorant," Luke answered. "Look, Betty was a decent woman with no husband and a couple of out-of-control boys as well as Carmen."

"Why didn't the state remove A.J. and Carmen?" Why was he defending the woman?

"Carmen wanted to stay. She wanted to help Betty. The state was probably grateful not to have to find another placement for A.J. Most foster families aren't in a big hurry to take in a teenage boy with a record and drug habit."

Julia turned to stir the food so that he wouldn't see the guilt in her eyes. "So, I know Carmen turned out okay. What about A.J. and the Andersons?"

"Betty's doing fine. Her hip bothers her when it rains, but—"

"Wait a minute," Julia interrupted, waving the wooden spoon, her heart in her throat. "Are you telling me you've stayed in touch with her even though you... even...after what happened?"

His dark brows arched and fell. "Other way around. She kept in touch with me," he explained. "Her letter to the judge is probably what kept me out of adult court."

Julia loved the woman already. "She sounds like a saint."

His lips twitched. "I think part of her motive was self-serving. I don't think she wanted anyone in her family or her church to know that Frank—among his other transgressions—beat her on a regular basis. I guess she figured he was gone and so was the problem. She's one of those head-in-the-sand types."

"Are you still in contact?"

"Occasionally, or whenever Carmen can swing it. My darling little foster sister suffers under the delusion that we should all forget the past, hold hands and sing 'Kumbaya.'"

Julia laughed. "And you?"

He blew out a long breath. "I have no problems with Betty. I'm trying tough love on A.J.—unsuccessfully, I might add. Tommy swears he's gotten his act together."

"You don't believe him?"

Luke's only response was to pull his lips into a taut line. "Whatever you're making smells great. I'm starving."

Okay, he was obviously done with the sharing part of the program. He'd revealed a lot of personal information she needed to digest. "Point me toward the plates and utensils so I can set the table."

"I'll do it," he offered, moving off the bench and joining her in the small galley. "You cooked."

His presence dominated the space as well

as her thoughts. She'd turned back to give the chicken a stir when she felt his solid body brush against her back. "Let me get out of your way," she suggested, loving the scent of him.

"I can reach."

He could, kind of. Because of the tight quarters and limited storage space, his body pressed against hers. Closing her eyes, she savored the feel of his warm, solid outline. Telling herself it would just be for a moment.

She expected to hear the clang of plates, though it would have been hard to hear anything above the pounding of her rapid pulse.

Luke gazed down just as her eyes fluttered open. Passion swirled in their smoky depths like an invitation. Curiosity got the better of him. He reached down, letting his finger trace the line of her jaw. Her skin was smooth and warm, like hot silk. Her breath came out in uneven puffs, spilling from slightly parted lips.

He couldn't quell the urge to kiss her. Didn't want to, actually. Couldn't think of one reason why he shouldn't.

Spinning her to the opposite side of the galley, he pulled her into the cradle of his thighs. Her palms flattened against his chest and he held his breath, afraid she might push him away. Afraid that she wouldn't.

Brushing a few strands of hair off her cheek, he gazed into her eyes. "Can that simmer or something?"

She nodded. "This probably isn't a good idea."

He smiled as he brushed his lips across her flushed forehead. "Well, things didn't work out when we *didn't* sleep together, so I think we should explore a different approach." Lifting the hair away from her neck, he dipped his head and kissed the smooth, floral-scented skin exposed. A sound, an erotic blend of a moan and a groan, rumbled in her throat.

Julia's arms looped around his neck as her head fell back. Encouraged, Luke dropped one hand to her waist while the other cupped her cheek. He tipped her head slightly, then worked his way to her mouth. Her moist breath heated his lips as they locked with hers.

His tongue stabbed into her mouth, testing and savoring the magic of her response. Need, real and palpable, surged through him. His body's reaction was fierce and predictable. Reaching around her, he fumbled for the knob on the stove, lowered the temperature on the burner, then swept her into his arms without ever breaking the kiss.

It was just a few short steps to his bed. Laying her gently atop the spread, he joined her, careful to balance some of his weight on his arms for fear of crushing her. He draped one leg over her thighs, pinning her to the mattress. He wanted to be so much closer. Dragging his mouth from hers, he peered down at her face. Her pupils were dilated, her breathing as fast and irregular as his own.

"Last chance," he said, bracing himself while he awaited her response.

Her answer was to reach for him, pulling his mouth to hers. Her hand slipped beneath his shirt. The sensation of her fingers massaging the muscles of his back was heady and only fueled the sense of urgency pounding in his veins.

Julia worked his shirt higher, tugging so hard he thought it might rip. Not that he cared. He, too, wanted nothing more than to feel her against him without barriers.

Completely enveloped in frenzied need, Luke slipped his hand beneath her shirt, seeking and finding the fullness of her breast encased in a lacy bra. He groaned into her mouth as he ran his finger over the outline of her pebbled nipple.

Deepening the kiss, he reached beneath her, deftly working the clasp. His pulse pounded in his ears as his hands roamed freely from breast to breast, exploring, needing the feel of her warm skin against his. He'd dreamed this scenario for the last six years, and the reality was more than he could have imagined.

In a rush of frantic pulling and tugging, shirts were removed and tossed to the floor. His gaze feasted on the perfection of her body. Her skin was bronze, flawless and flushed. His breath caught in his chest as his eyes settled on her breasts, swollen and heavy with passion. He kissed her collarbone, drawing his tongue lower until he took her peaked nipple in his mouth. She gasped and arched against him as her fingernails dug into his shoulders.

Sliding his palm along her side, he brushed the outline of her hipbone through her slacks. With his own body straining against his pants, he shifted, his fingers searching desperately for the zipper.

"Luke!" He was taken aback by the change in her voice. It was higher in pitch and strangely distant. Conscious thought spiraled through the thick fog of passion until comprehension finally dawned. Hell.

Julia heard a vaguely familiar female voice call for Luke again, and it took her desire-addled brain a few seconds to realize it wasn't hers. She shoved him away, nearly flinging him to the ground as she scrambled off the bed and started groping around the floor for her clothing.

"Luke?"

"Hang on," he growled.

Apology was etched in the look he gave Julia as he shrugged into his shirt and bolted out of the cabin.

Well. If that wasn't enough to make a girl cry, she didn't know what was. Was it her destiny to never have sex with Luke Young? While she dressed, Julia bobbed her head and peered out the oval window. Luke had intercepted Carmen and was leading her back up the dock.

They were too far away for her to hear their conversation, but it was very, very animated. Carmen planted her hands on her hips and got right up in Luke's face. In response, he shook his head a few times. They went back and forth like that for several minutes.

Julia finger-combed her hair as she continued to watch the heated encounter. Curiosity curbed the passion still tingling in her nerve endings. Was it an argument or just a lively exchange?

Maybe, if she went into the galley, she'd be able to eavesdrop enough to get the gist of the conversation. She had just stepped out there when a telephone perched on one of the shelves began to ring. She moved toward it, annoyed that the phone lacked caller ID. It did, however, have an answering machine that clicked on in screen mode.

"You have reached Young Construction. Leave a message."

Beep.

"You owe me," a chilling, digitally altered voice said. "Now it's time to pay."

Chapter Ten

The blood stilled in Julia's veins, clearing her head of residual lust. Remembering her assignment, she grabbed the phone as soon as the message recorded, and pressed *69.

"Not a subscriber," a mechanical voice announced. Frustration gripped her. Did Luke have to be the only person on the planet who didn't have bundled phone service?

As she contemplated her next move, he returned, anger simmering in his dark eyes.

"Problem?" she asked, hoping she didn't have guilt written all over her.

"Nothing major." He rubbed his hands over his face, then offered a sheepish grin. "Since you're dressed, I'm guessing the, er, moment is over, right?"

"Good guess."

He took a step in her direction. "Let's see if I can change your mind."

She held up her hands and shot him a warning look. "I think we both know you could, so don't."

"Don't ever, or just not right now?"

Cocking her head, she studied him briefly. "What is it with you and absolutes? You're not much of a go-with-the-flow kind of guy, are you?"

"I don't like surprises," he readily admitted.

"Neither do I, but I just got a doozy."

"Doozy?" he repeated with a deep, resonating chuckle. "I didn't think people used that word anymore."

"Before you mock me, I suggest you listen to the message."

The slightest bit of color drained from his face. She could almost hear the wheels turning inside his head.

It was telling that he didn't race to the machine. As if he already knew what to expect.

"Who's your creepy caller?" she asked.

"Smells good. Why don't we eat?" He brushed past her, making a production out of gathering plates and utensils.

Julia grabbed his elbow, forcing him to stand still. Her gaze locked with his. "Tell me about these calls."

He sighed heavily and gave a little shrug. "It's nothing. A.J. owes some of the wrong people money. They're under the mistaken impression that I'll cover his debts."

"That wasn't what it sounded like to me."

"Don't worry about it, Julia. I'm handling it."

"Really? How? Since you aren't surprised, I take it this isn't the first call?"

He pulled free of her hold. "No, it isn't the first. It's really not a big deal. Drop it."

She balled her hands into tight fists at her sides. "Not a big deal? We were shot at, remember?"

His dark eyes bored into her. "I'm the one with his head glued together, so yes, I remember it."

"Did you share any of this with the police?"

"A.J.'s butt is already in a sling. I didn't want to jam him up." Luke let out a long sigh. Fatigue settled over his features.

It was moments like this, moments when he was vulnerable and totally *Luke,* that tugged at her heartstrings. For the second time, he was her assignment, nothing more. Intellectually, that was fine. But intellect wasn't constricting her heart. It wasn't what fueled her guilt or drove her passion.

In a cruel turn of fate, the feelings she kept so deeply buried then were just as strong as ever now. And again the situation was impossible. Her hands were tied; she had no choice but to keep up the pretext. To keep telling herself that she wasn't in love with him.

Saying the words, even if only in her head, came with a bolt of searing pain straight to her heart. Her whole world seemed to be about "if onlys."

If only they could find Sonya and return her safely to Juan and her family.

If only Uncle Carlos hadn't suffered a stroke.

If only Julia could be honest with Luke.

She gave herself a little mental shake. Wanting wasn't getting, so she had to focus. "Are the calls the reason you've been so accepting of the shooting in front of Weddings Your Way? I mean, you've hardly mentioned it. No questions, nothing."

"A.J.'s dealer doesn't want me dead, he wants me to pay. Killing me wouldn't achieve that objective, now would it?"

"Automatic weapons are a favorite with drug dealers."

One dark brow cocked above his pointed

stare. "You're a seamstress *and* an expert on weapons?"

She forced her voice to remain even. "Expert enough to know that we were shot at with some pretty intense firepower."

"What do you want me to say?" he growled. "That I almost got you killed a second time?"

"What?"

"The Esterhaus thing was my fault." As he said it, pain flashed in his eyes. "Do you have any idea how it felt to know I'd put you in danger?"

You bet I do. Damn, he blamed himself? "Esterhaus wasn't your fault. That's crazy, Luke."

He vehemently shook his head. "Why do you think I went to that home show in Vegas?"

She leaned against the counter, her mind slipping pieces into place, even as her body chilled. "You knew Esterhaus was a drug trafficker?"

"I suspected," he admitted.

"How?"

"A.J.," he said, clearly pained by the admission. "One of Esterhaus's distributors was trying to recruit A.J. so they could expand their operation in south Florida.

Using is bad enough. Selling that junk would have put A.J. in a whole new league. I couldn't just stand by and let that happen to him."

"What was your plan?"

"I knew from A.J. that Esterhaus needed a new way to import the drugs. A way to fly under the customs radar. A lieutenant from Esterhaus's crew knew about my construction company and that A.J. often works for me. During one of his clean periods, A.J. told me about the proposal, so I decided to intervene."

"Well that was incredibly dumb," she said, jaw clenched. "Why didn't you go to the authorities with your information? They could have helped you—"

"Help me what?" he said with a sneer. "In the drug world, it was common knowledge that Esterhaus was untouchable. He'd been arrested several times, but the charges never stuck. I didn't think they'd be much help."

"Given how things turned out, you were wrong."

He gave a slight shrug. "I didn't talk to the DEA and they didn't consult me. Look, it doesn't matter. The end result is Esterhaus is in prison. You weren't hurt. It all worked out."

"Except that A.J.'s still a junkie and his dealer is all over you."

Luke tucked his thumbs into his front pockets and drawled, "I hardly think you're in a position to criticize me. The shooting at Weddings Your Way could just as easily be related to the Botero kidnapping."

Point. She drew herself up to her full height, determined to make him back down. "Well, I think it's time for you to put away your Dick Tracy decoder ring and let the professionals handle this."

Her remark coaxed a wry smile from him. "This from the woman whose apartment was destroyed by C-4?"

She was stunned and it must have shown on her face, because he said, "Yes, I know that whole gas leak thing was garbage. I've worked in construction my whole adult life, Julia. I know what C-4 smells like. I figured your boss wouldn't let you say anything. I'm guessing Weddings Your Way can't afford any more bad publicity. I also knew *you* knew because you've been so nonchalant about it."

What could she say that wouldn't make her look like a liar? How could she protect her job and her heart at the same time?

He shrugged. "That would be the only sensible explanation for your behavior the last couple of days. You could have told me. It's not like I'm going to rat you out to your boss or anything. I wouldn't jeopardize your job, but I want you to start thinking seriously about your safety."

This conversation had crossed over into the surreal. He wanted to protect her? "Meaning?"

He rose and took two long strides, reaching out and taking her hands in his. He gazed down at her with so much care and concern in his eyes that she wanted desperately to blurt out the truth. She wanted to put him at ease, let him know she was fully capable of handling any situation. Tell him everything about her years with the DEA and her current position with Miami Confidential. Mostly she wanted to tell him that she was falling in love with him.

His hand came up, cupping her cheek gently as he brushed a kiss on her forehead. Instantly, her body stirred. She was filled with longing and need. She wanted him more than her next breath. So much so that it scared her in ways bullets and bombs never could.

"I want you out of harm's way," he said, his lips tickling her skin. "Cut me some slack here. Carmen already gave me grief *and* she interrupted us."

For which I'm eternally grateful, Julia thought. Sleeping with Luke would add another, unwelcome layer of complexity to a situation that seemed to be spiraling out of her control.

Resting her hands on his waist, Julia leaned into his embrace. She breathed in the soothing scent of him. Felt the warmth of his body as she listened to the even, rhythmic beat of his heart.

Luke stroked her hair with one hand and placed the other at the small of her back. She felt safe, cherished, and wished this moment could last forever. Sadly, she knew it couldn't.

Even if she was free to tell him about her job, it wouldn't negate the fact that she'd lied to him from the start. She needed to stop this.

Long ago, she'd chosen her work over everything else. It was her focus. What mattered most. She was doing good things. Things that helped real people in need. She wasn't used to being one of those people, particularly when her needs were purely emotional, not to mention irrational. The sooner she put her feelings back in their box, the better off she'd be.

"So," she began as she slipped out of his hold. "Why did Carmen give you grief?" She began dishing chicken onto their plates.

"Same debate, different day," he told her as they sat diagonally from one another at the compact table.

"What's the problem?" she asked, watching as he tasted the first bite of food.

"Mandatory Monday dinner. This is fabulous," he exclaimed. "You'll have to teach me to make it. On second thought," he added, fork poised in the air, "don't teach me. Stick around so you can make it whenever the spirit moves you."

"I work next door," she said, dancing around the open invitation and its implications. "I suppose I could drop by every now and again." She didn't know why she teased, "What's in it for me?"

His response came in the form of an explicit glimmer in his eyes.

Julia let out a little laugh. When had she learned how to flirt? "Beyond the obvious. I *suppose* we could barter."

"For what?"

"Tell me about Monday dinner and maybe throw in some sailing lessons," she suggested. "I'd love to learn."

"I'd love to teach you to sail. And I'll do you one better on Monday dinner." He paused. "Come with me."

"Excuse me?"

"Yeah," he said, his tone gaining enthusiasm. "Be my date."

"That's hardly appropriate under the circumstances."

"What circumstances?"

"I work for Carmen and Dalton, and besides, I'm sure the three of you probably have—I don't know—*family* things to do. It wouldn't be appropriate for me to be there."

The corners of his mouth turned down as he scowled. "Welcome to the club. Dalton won't be eating with us. Carmen just informed me that in addition to me and A.J., the Andersons are going to be there."

Julia felt her eyes widen. "Is that going to be awkward for you?"

"Considering the history, yes."

"Then why is she doing it?"

"Carmen wants me to get to know Dalton better, and I guess she just wants to see for herself that Tommy and I can be civil to one another before the actual wedding."

"Can you?"

"Sure. It's always comfortable for me to be in the same room with the family of the man I killed," he answered sarcastically.

Julia put her fork down, finished with her meal. "Can't you get out of it?"

"No. Carmen is insisting and I have a hard time saying no to her. A fact," he added with a self-deprecating grin, "she is keenly aware of and takes advantage of whenever possible."

"Really?"

He nodded. "On top of rehabbing this marina and the yacht club, Carmen snagged me to do some stuff around Dalton's house."

"Why? I hear it's a showplace." When he gave her a questioning look, she added, "Nicole, she's the photographer for Weddings Your Way, went over to do their engagement portraits. She said the place was stunning."

He shrugged. "If you happen to like lots of gilded fixtures, gilded mirrors and ornate gilded statuary. Carmen doesn't, so she wants me to redo the bathrooms and replace some of the electrical stuff. What I really think is she wants to make it *their* home, not his."

"That stands to reason," Julia agreed once

she thought about it. "I'd hate to feel like a guest in my own home."

"You don't have a home, remember?"

She frowned. "I hate the idea of having to find another apartment. Aside from the fact that it takes a lot of time—time I definitely don't have during bride month—I never seem to find anything I really like."

He pushed his empty plate aside and glanced down at his watch before leaning back against the seat cushion. "June is bride month?"

"For the most part, though that's changing. Still, there are enough women who insist on being June brides that my schedule gets a little crazy this time of year."

"What kind of home would you really like?" he asked.

"Nothing that fits in my budget," she answered.

"Your fantasy, then."

You're my fantasy, but you don't fit into my emotional budget. Deciding to be truthful, especially since it couldn't hurt, she answered, "I really like simple beach cottages. You know, sherbet-colored stucco, plantation shutters, blah, blah, blah. I'd love to be able to hear the ocean at night. Then again, I'd have to win the lottery to be able to afford a place on the beach. Even if I could afford the location, most of those homes are older and I'm not very handy."

"How many bedrooms?"

"Two. Maybe three," she said, closing her eyes and picturing her dream home. "A modest pool would be nice. Nothing fancy, a basic oval with a small sundeck." She could see herself on a lounger, basking in warmth.

"Kitchen?"

Her eyes opened as she blurted easily, "State of the art. I'd want all the cool things I see on those home makeover shows. I'd really love one of those built-in grills. Oh, and a dishwasher that doesn't sound like Sherman's army is approaching."

"New construction or rehab?" he asked as he started clearing the dishes.

"Renovated, I think. I'd like something that has all that old-fashioned charm but all the bells and whistles of current technology."

"Sounds doable."

She stiffened, surprised at how much she'd revealed. "I don't care how it sounds, it's not an option. I don't have the time or the money."

"Depends on how much you want it and how long you're willing to wait."

"Says the King of I Must Have All My Ducks in a Row," she teased.

He turned, his dark head lowered so she couldn't quite read his eyes. "Speaking of lining things up, let's discuss what you're going to do until you find a place."

"No need," she explained. "My car is loaded with enough stuff to get me through the next week or so. There's a cot and a shower at Weddings Your Way, so I figured I could just stay there for a while."

"I want you to stay here."

She bit her tongue before she just blurted out "yes!" then cast him a suspicious glance. "To play house with you?"

His grin was slow and sensual. "Actually, we'd be playing boat, not house."

"Same difference." Her cheeks heated.

"Okay," he said, raising his hands in mock surrender. "As much as I'd love to share my boat and my bed with you, how about this? You can have the stern cabin."

That would make protecting him easier. At the cost of opening her heart to danger. "That's a very generous offer, but—"

"I insist. Besides, it benefits us both."

"How?"

"You get free digs and I get to spend more

time with you." He checked his watch again. "But not right now. I've got to go meet the developer."

"Where?"

She saw a glint spring into his eyes. "Here on site. Will you miss me?"

Dodging his outstretched hand, she side-stepped his attempt to draw her into his arms. "Believe it or not, I have work to do as well. We're putting on a wedding tomorrow, so I've got some last minute nips and tucks to oversee."

"So meet me back here when you're done. We'll grab dinner."

"I don't know how long I'll be," she hedged. What would Rachel say?

"Doesn't matter," he insisted, opening one of the galley drawers and taking out a leather portfolio. "Whenever you get here is fine. We can talk about Monday night's dinner disaster."

"I don't think I should go. I can't intrude like that." Of course, it would give her the best chance at protecting him.

He started for the deck, pausing to run the pad of his forefinger along the side of her face. Julia's body gave a little shiver as anticipation and desire pooled within her. How could he do that with just a touch? His finger hooked beneath her chin, lifting her face.

He showered her with tiny kisses, nibbled her earlobe and ran his lips along the side of her throat. Julia moaned softly, swimming in sensations. This wasn't like earlier in the day. Not hard and fast and greedy. This was slow and gentle, as if he was savoring every second of the adept way his mouth explored hers. It was even more devastating to her senses.

Yes, the passion was there. But this kiss was different. It heated her all over, the warmth finally settling in her heart. Yes, this kiss was dangerous. It confirmed her deepest fears.

"Julia?" he whispered against her mouth.

If he told her he loved her—hell, *liked* her would do—she'd melt right there. "Yes?"

"I've got to go."

"Okay," she murmured reluctantly.

"It would be easier to do if you'd let go of my waist."

She did, leaping backward into the edge of table. She almost lost her footing along with her dignity. "H-have a good…"

"Meet-ing," he said in carefully separated syllables.

The sound of his amused chuckle reverberated in her ears, leaving her feeling dazed and tingly.

Julia watched him as he strode down the dock in the direction of the yacht club. Not taking her eyes off Luke, she reached for her cell phone to call Jeff. He could take over for a while. He'd protect Luke from whomever was threatening him.

Now, if only she could call someone who could protect her from herself.

Chapter Eleven

"When was the call?" Rachel asked.

Julia glanced over at the clock on her desk. "About three hours ago."

Rachel was unflappable, her expression almost impossible to decipher.

It didn't help that Julia's insides were twisted into a huge knot. It was difficult to judge another person's reactions when she was struggling to maintain her own focus.

The intercom buzzed. It was Vicki, the receptionist, alerting them about an incoming fax on the secure line.

Julia followed her boss into the conference room.

The scent of coffee called to her. This whole sleep deprivation thing was getting old. There was a time when Julia could do surveillance all night, then run an obstacle course after her shift. Obviously, those days were waning.

For the first time ever, she wondered about her future. The reality was, her job demanded a fair amount of physical stamina. If a few sleepless nights had her dragging now, what would happen when she was forty? Fifty?

She loved her job, believed in what they did, and genuinely cared about the clients. Still, she wanted more. More responsibility, more control. That would only happen if she got her own branch office.

She filled a mug with thin, pale coffee, grimacing when she tasted the pathetically weak brew. "This is like light brown water," she remarked. Focusing on the coffee seemed like a better alternative than thinking about her career crossroads. If she got her own branch, she'd have to relocate. Until a few days ago, when Luke walked back into her life, that would have been all well and good.

Careful what you wish for, her brain taunted. She'd spent the better part of the last year bucking for a promotion. Now she was rethinking that goal. A new position would mean leaving Luke. Again. Assuming he would even be interested in her after all of this was over. What would he think about her real job? Could she ever tell him, and if she couldn't, would it be fair to him, giving him only a part of herself? She knew that when it came to Luke, she wanted it all. Didn't he deserve the same?

The whole confusing scenario filled her with a tangible sorrow that seemed to settle over her like a dark cloud.

"Sit," Rachel instructed, pointing to the chair directly to her left. She held a disorganized stack of pages fresh off the fax machine. Rachel's half-glasses dangled between her thumb and forefinger. She regarded Julia for several long, uncomfortable seconds. "Want to tell me what's going on?"

"The status report I gave you earlier was—"

"I'm not asking for the official version," Rachel interrupted. Annoyance shone in her sparkling blue eyes. "This is coming as a friend, now, not your boss."

"Nothing I can't handle," Julia hedged. Admitting any sort of weakness to Rachel could cost her in the long run. She'd never been foolish enough to confuse the line between friend and boss, anyway.

"You look like someone just kicked your dog."

"I don't have a dog."

"C'mon," Rachel insisted. "We either

have a brief off-the-record chat or we have to have a very long on-the-record discussion. Your choice."

Julia folded her hands in her lap and stared abstractedly at her chipped thumbnail, but she didn't speak right away. She was afraid to say anything and just as afraid not to. She blew a frustrated breath in the general direction of her forehead.

"You and Luke?" Rachel prodded. "Is there a problem?"

"Yeah." This was gonna bite her in the butt, even if it was the right thing to do. "Me."

"Want off the assignment?" Rachel asked neutrally.

"No," Julia answered without hesitation. "There's probably no one else on the face of the earth who's got more of a vested interest in keeping Luke safe than I do."

"I thought so," Rachel said, her tone filled with amusement.

That caused Julia's head to whip up. "Did I miss something?"

"Apparently. We'll drop it for now," Rachel said, slipping on her glasses. "Before we get to this…" she paused, fluttering the pages "...I'll bring you up to speed on the Botero situation."

Her attention fully focused, Julia gripped the arms of her chair tightly.

"Craig Johnson was poisoned with an injection of atropine. It's a drug used to jump-start the heart when it stops. It mimics a heart attack when it's given to a healthy person. He's in a coma, but he'll make it."

That news, filtered through her anger, was both a blessing and a curse. "When he comes out of it, can I kill him? Slowly?"

"You'll have to stand in line," Rachel stated wryly. "Rafe has already called dibs and I think he's behind the Botero's security chief, Sean Majors."

"Any leads on why he betrayed Sonya like that?" Julia asked.

"Money, probably. The lab tests are back on the ransom note. It was Sonya's blood."

Julia felt her throat constrict. "So what's the next step?"

"Sophie is working with Botero's security guy. We've got it covered."

"Still no idea where Sonya's being held?"

Rachel shook her head. A few strands of ebony hair fell loose to frame her face. As usual, she was dressed to perfection, in a gauzy skirt and pale cream top accessorized with lots of chunky jewelry. It always amazed Julia that her boss could manage to look so great regardless of the day or the occasion.

"The lab found several grains of pollen in the sample you got." Rachel paused for a little laugh. "I have this mental image of you improvising a lab in the ladies' room and it amuses me to no end. You're a terrific agent, able to think fast in any situation."

Julia soaked up the praise, needing it after she'd made the biggest mistake of her career. Falling for her "assignment."

"Anyway, we're sending it out to a botanist to see if that helps us."

Julia's mood grew solemn. "Do you think Sonya is still alive?"

"Absolutely," Rachel answered. "She's of no use to them dead. If the kidnappers want money, they wouldn't dare kill her until they collect. If, on the other hand, this was a message for Juan from the Laderan drug cartel, they'd have killed Sonya outright."

"Did Ethan get to Ladera yet?"

Rachel nodded. "Landed a few hours ago. I'm waiting now for a webcast. He's meeting Juan's first wife, Maggie, at the sanatorium. Probably a dead end, but I don't want any detail overlooked. Have you checked on Mr. Botero?"

"Yes. He wants to be released." Julia smiled. Thinking of how well he was doing eased some of the tension that had settled between her shoulders. "Swears he can recover much faster in the comfort of his own home."

"He's probably right," Rachel acknowledged. "With his money, he can afford private care. Hell, he can afford to build his own personal hospital. But for your sake, I'm glad he's doing so well."

"He's got some residual weakness on his left side." Julia lifted one shoulder. "With exercise and rehab, he'll make a near-complete recovery. *If* he follows orders and *if* the stress of Sonya still missing doesn't cause a second stroke."

"Think positively, Julia."

"I'm trying, but it's hard," she admitted, taking another sip of the lukewarm, watered down coffee. "Anything show up on the hospital surveillance of Craig Johnson's room?"

Rachel sighed. "The images are grainy. Nicole is running the copies through the digital image enhancement program. She says it will take time for the computer to sharpen the picture because of ghost images."

"Excuse me?" Julia said, swallowing the urge to laugh as her boss fumbled through the technology jargon. "She saw ghosts?"

Rachel waved her hand dismissively, making the bracelets on her wrist jingle. "Something along those lines. Apparently the hospital uses the same tapes over and over again. The old images are never completely erased, so they leave 'ghost' images. And the...the computer is afraid of ghosts, I guess. Ask Nicole, she's the technology whiz as well as the photographer."

"Is there anything I can do?" Julia asked.

"The Botero matter is covered. Moving on, I've gathered a lot of background on Mr. Young as well as the people he's closest to. Let's see what we can do for your Luke."

He isn't mine. The realization made her sad. It was ridiculous. Every stumbling block in their relationship could be traced directly back to one of her lies.

"Albert Jason Taggert, aka A. J. Taggert. Twenty-six years old. Father unknown. Alcoholic mother who had several arrests for solicitation, public intoxication and disturbing the peace. Lost custody of her son when he was three, died when he was eight. No other living relatives, so he was made a ward of the state. Four different placements before landing with the Anderson family when he was eight."

Julia felt a tug at her heart. From the background report it sounded as if A.J. was pretty much damned in the womb.

Rachel continued, "Expelled from the seventh grade for pulling a knife on his English teacher after she reminded him that his homework was late. Arrests for shoplifting, B and E, resisting arrest, assault on a police officer, possession of stolen goods, possession of a controlled substance, possession of drug paraphernalia." Rachel removed her glasses. "Sounds like A.J. is in possession of everything but a moral compass and some common sense."

"Known associates?" Julia asked, figuring it was easier to treat A.J. like a job instead of Luke's foster brother.

Rachel held her glasses in front of her face, but didn't actually put them on. "He was arrested three times with Thomas Anderson. Once on breaking and entering and the other two for drugs."

Poor Luke. "Recently?"

Rachel shook her head. "Anderson's been a good boy for the last five years. Drug-free for the last three months. A.J. is another story. Six arrests during the same time period. The last one was eleven months ago."

"What's the disposition on that case?"

"Plea agreement pending. Mandatory thirty-day drug rehab. Translation—the state must want him to flip on his drug connection. Probably need him to build a case on someone else. That's the only logical reason for the plea and an explanation for why he wasn't slapped with a parole violation as well."

Luke certainly had his hands full. "What about the Andersons?"

Rachel leaned back in her chair, propping her fingers together beneath her chin. "The information is a little sketchy on Frank. Betty had several visits to the ER over the years. Always claimed she'd fallen or tripped."

"No one ever intervened?"

"Several doctors asked about abuse, but she always denied it. One in particular wanted to call in the police, but after Betty explained about the foster children in her care, he dropped it."

Anger simmered just below the surface. Julia loathed men who vented their personal frustrations with their fists. "Frank?"

"Yes, to a point."

Julia frowned. "Meaning?"

"Betty has been back to the ER twice since Frank was killed. Both times for broken arms."

"Do we have any details?"

"One time she claimed she slipped in her own driveway on the way to the mailbox. In the second incident, three years ago, she said she fell off her bike."

"You sound skeptical."

"I had Vicki check the satellite maps. Betty Anderson had a dirt driveway."

"So, she was lying. What about the second incident?"

"The bike riding thing sounds fishy. How many women do you know who take up cycling in their sixties?"

"It does happen," Julia reasoned with a frown. "She could have been trying to lose weight or keep her cholesterol down, fend off a heart attack or any number of other reasons."

"Maybe," Rachel hedged. "If someone was hurting her after Frank died, A.J. is the most likely candidate. By all accounts, he's got a pretty volatile temper, especially when he's under the influence. I'm working on getting copies of the original medical records. Perhaps those can shed some light on what was going on in that house."

"Luke invited me to dinner on Monday. The Andersons will be there."

"Then go," Rachel insisted. "Check them out. My gut tells me there's something hinky about that family."

"Hinky doesn't begin to cover it," Julia insisted. "I don't get why they stay in touch." She stood, pacing the room. "From Luke's description, Frank was mean and abusive. Betty was a wounded, helpless bird. Luke accidentally killed Frank, but it's Betty who rushed to his defense and even visited him when he was in prison. There's something not right about that."

"What about the other children? Do you have a feel for that dynamic?" Rachel asked.

Julia stopped pacing, then braced her hands on the back of the chair. "I think Luke is the fixer. Carmen is the peacemaker. They're really close. A.J. is obviously the screwup. Tommy claims to have reformed, but I get the feeling Luke isn't totally convinced. Tommy was a jerk who may or may not have turned it around. Luke doesn't say much about Betty, but I know he feels remorse for killing her husband, even though Frank was a creep and it was an accident."

"Court records indicate that both Tommy and A.J. spiraled out of control after Frank's death," Rachel stated.

Julia shrugged, thinking that might be normal. Except they took it to the extreme. "I'll know more after Monday."

One of Rachel's perfectly shaped brows arched. "Until then?"

"Hopefully, we can get more information on A.J. and—"

"No," Rachel interrupted. "I was talking about you. What are you going to do until then?"

"Jeff and I are sharing surveillance. I'd like to get a tap on Luke's phone ASAP."

"It will be in place before the end of the day." Rachel pursed her lips, then seemed to measure her words as she asked, "Are you sleeping with him?"

"No." *Not for lack of trying.*

"Planning to?"

Defensively, Julia replied, "It's not in my week-at-a-glance."

A glint of amusement flickered in Rachel's unwavering gaze. "Maybe not, but I have a feeling this guy is different. The two of you have a history."

"*Bad* history," Julia reminded her. "Don't worry, Rachel, I know my primary allegiance is to Miami Confidential."

Her boss's brow furrowed deeply. "Your work is important, Julia, but that doesn't mean you don't get to have a life. Look at Samantha."

She did think about Samantha, about how much happier she was since she'd found Alex Graham. It only added to Julia's inner turmoil. She had put thoughts of a "normal" life out of her mind for so long, she wasn't sure she even knew how to blend personal and professional anymore.

Not that she'd had a lot of opportunities. Aside from the long hours her job demanded, there was the whole secrecy thing. "Samantha is the exception," Julia pointed out, in no great hurry to reassess her priorities. Even if she could risk it, Luke would never understand or forgive her once he discovered the extent of her deception. Her heart stung at the thought.

She knew, absolutely knew, that he'd never buy her justifications. He was nothing if not absolute. He would never understand her motives or her world.

"Want to watch the webcast from Ladera?" Rachel asked. "Or would you rather stand there looking like you're planning your own demise?"

"Webcast," Julia answered, shoving the self-pity out of her mind.

She followed the vapor trail of Rachel's designer perfume into the narrow computer room through the pocket door. The windowless area was flooded with harsh light from long, tubular fluorescent rods mounted along the edge of the ceiling.

A long counter supported no fewer than a dozen computers, scanners and assorted other state-of-the-art pieces of equipment. Above those, flat panel monitors in varying sizes were mounted on the walls.

A cluster of ten stadium-style seats created a two-tiered viewing area. Sophie Brooks and Nicole O'Shae were already seated, though Sophie stood and automatically relinquished the primo seat to Rachel. Nicole had a cordless keyboard balanced in her lap.

"Hi, Julia. How's it going?" Nicole asked.

Julia sidestepped into the back row, sitting directly behind Nicole as she mumbled some innocuous answer, then exchanged greetings with her other colleague. Nicole's nimble fingers flew across the keyboard, stopping only once to adjust the black, spiky choker adorning her neck. Nicole was nothing if not an individual.

Julia kept her eyes and attention fixed on the images flickering on the large center screen. Well, she tried. While adjustments were made to strengthen the signal, her mind veered off track.

Her feelings for Luke were a potential problem. *Potential?* the little voice in her head challenged. Okay, so they were a big problem. Huge if she acknowledged that loving him wasn't a possibility. It had sneaked up on her and become a reality.

The clarity of that thought stunned her. Julia raked her fingers through her hair, wondering how she could have let this happen. Six years ago, she'd chalked it all up to the excitement of her first big case.

Now she was forced to admit that wasn't the truth. She couldn't claim it was the result of being shocked at seeing him again. Nor did her feelings relate to the shooting, the bombing or even the threats. Yes, she was more emotional than normal because Sonya was still out there suffering God-only-knew what. But even that upheaval couldn't explain the purely instinctual attraction pulling Julia toward the one man she could never have.

"Getting this?" Ethan Whitehawk's voice thundered from the overhead speakers as clearly as if he was sitting right there in the room.

Rachel took a wireless mike from inside the armrest compartment. "Crystal clear," she told him.

Ethan's voice was deep, his tone brusque. Much like the man, Julia thought as his image flashed in her brain. Ethan was part Native American, with black hair, chiseled, nearly perfect features and brooding brown eyes that conveyed nothing. He'd spent most of his career investigating crimes on reservations in the U.S. Among his many skills, Ethan was a master at gathering information.

Because of his mixed ethnicity, Ethan had a chameleonlike ability to blend into any number of cultures. Julia was sure he already had the Laderans thinking he was a local.

Judging by the sway of the images, Julia guessed Ethan was using the nifty little watch cam. In full, vivid color, she got her first glimpse of Ladera. Though Sonya had regaled her with stories of her visits there with Juan, Julia was ill-prepared for the lush beauty of the place.

"Are those for real?" Nicole asked, obviously impressed by images of a stunning walkway lineá with huge yellow blossoms.

Ethan replied, "Yes." He angled the camera to pan up to a mosaic sign that read Hospital de los Problemes de los Inocentes.

The other women looked to Julia for a translation. "Hospital for Problems of the Innocent," she supplied.

"Mental institution," she clarified, understanding that literal translations often made little or no sense. Secretly, she also thought that her native language was preferable. English was specific, succinct and absolute, leaving very little room for nuances.

A lot like Luke.

Gnashing her teeth, she silently hoped her fixation on that man would let up soon. She was turning into a pitiful cliché of a morose lover. She and Luke could never be together in any meaningful way. The sooner she wrapped her brain around that reality, the better off she'd be.

Ethan provided them with a panorama view of the sanatorium. It looked more like a hotel than a private institution. No, Julia amended to herself as he walked inside the arched courtyard. It looked like a spa.

Soothing colors, fresh flowers and lots and lots of staff milled around in attractively tailored uniforms.

"I'm Dr. Whitehawk from the Global Research Center." He slipped a badge across a polished marble counter. "I have clearance to interview Maggie DeLeon."

"Nice job," Julia murmured, patting Nicole on the shoulder.

"A simple create and laminate," Nicole joked. "Making the ID was easy. You should have seen the letterhead I made for Global Research. By the time I finished even *I* thought they were a legit organization."

"Please follow me," the receptionist said.

Ethan's walk down the hall revealed even more impressive details. The hospital where Juan's ex-wife lived was better than most five-star hotels.

The first image of Maggie DeLeon was surprising. Julia had expected some pathetic patient drugged to the gills, wearing a bathrobe and drooling on herself. The woman she saw on the monitor was nothing like that.

She was stunning, perfectly coiffed and seated in a cushioned wicker chair on the veranda just off her room. Her clothing was equally perfect, and even via webcast, Julia recognized an air of dignity about her.

Maggie smiled and extended her hand. The smile didn't reach her eyes. Possibly because she was medicated, or emotionally disconnected as a result of her psychotic break.

Sonya had shared bits and pieces about her fiancé's ex. Maggie's drug overdose had cost her everything—her baby, her marriage, her faculties and very nearly her life.

Ethan began asking her questions, starting with the basics, then moving on to Juan.

"He doesn't visit me anymore," Maggie said, her eyes fixed off in the distance. "Did you know that he pursued me for nearly six months before I agreed to marry him?" Her hand moved sluggishly up to smooth her hair. "I had many suitors."

"But do you know where Sonya Botero is?" Nicole blurted out impatiently.

After another twenty minutes it became clear that either Maggie DeLeon was a great actress or she didn't know anything about Sonya's kidnapping.

"She drifts off during thoughts," Samantha said. "Changes topics erratically. Lacks the ability to stay focused. Textbook symptoms of cognitive impairment."

"How textbook?" Julia asked. "Could she be faking?"

"Of course," Samantha answered. "If she is, she's very well coached. Given that she didn't know Ethan would show up to interview her until ten hours ago, I don't see how she could be this well prepared to fake an illness."

"So, we're nowhere?" Rachel asked, exasperation in her tone.

"Can you pause that and play it back?" Julia interrupted, catching something on-screen.

Nicole obliged, stopping the real-time feed, rewinding, then picking up with the last couple of questions and answers.

"Maggie, do you like it here?"

"It's okay," she answered without affect. "I don't have so many friends."

"But you do have visitors, right?"

She nodded stiffly. "My cousin Roberto, other family. On the weekends. Ramon makes sure to put out fresh flowers when they visit."

"Ramon?" Julia repeated, recognizing the name. She grabbed a mike. "Ethan, ask about Ramon."

Nicole put the feed back on real time.

"Who is Ramon?" Ethan asked. "Does he work here?"

Maggie nodded.

"Is he a nurse? An orderly? What does he do for you?"

She smiled and waved her hand dismissively. Julia noticed that the first Mrs. DeLeon still wore her wedding band. "No, he's an important man. He's my doctor."

Chapter Twelve

Julia remembered the string of numbers she'd found, what felt like a lifetime ago, in Craig Johnson's wallet, and the bizarre call to "Ramon," a "farmer." Yeah, right. "So how does a doctor from a Laderan mental institution get calls forwarded to Miami? And why claim to be a farmer? Why pay a chauffeur to kidnap Sonya?" Julia murmured to herself as she sat in her work area, tacking lace onto the bodice of Carmen's wedding dress.

As she made the tiny, next-to-invisible stitches, she considered the possibilities. Maggie DeLeon was beautiful. Men often did stupid things to impress women they loved. And Maggie was still wearing her wedding band.... Did she even realize that she wasn't married anymore? Perhaps, due to her mental state, she believed herself still wed to the man of her dreams. And because of her illness, was it possible that the doctors let her continue believing it?

Or maybe Ramon himself had fallen in love with the tragically lovely Maggie and figured if he kidnapped Sonya, he'd destroy Juan. And once Juan was out of the picture it might clear the way for him in Maggie's heart.

Julia looked up from her work as she murmured, "Or maybe he blames Juan for abandoning Maggie and it's about vengeance?" No, none of that made much sense, she decided. It was overcomplicated. In her experience, the motivation for most crimes was simple and straightforward. Love, money, revenge, power.

The repetitive act of sewing stitch after stitch helped her to think. Ethan was going to track down the doctor, so until then, she'd have to be patient. While Sonya would be…what? Terrified, Julia knew. Her heart ached for her friend.

Her heart ached for another reason, too. Glancing up at the clock, she realized it was close to nine. She should probably call Luke and beg off. "Take the chicken's way out," she whispered with a humorless laugh.

It was only Tuesday and she already had the bodice finished, all she had left to do before the wedding were the alterations to the tuxes. She surveyed her work, envisioning Carmen on what was supposed to be the happiest day of a woman's life. The bride would be beautiful, Julia thought with a sigh as she set the dress aside. There was nothing more to occupy her time, since she was ahead of schedule. She had no excuse not to call Luke, which made her antsy as all get-out.

Going back into her office, she was stunned to find Luke sitting in her chair. Her heart skipped a beat before she asked, "What are you doing here?"

He flashed a bone-melting smile as he stood and pulled her into his arms before she had time to protest. "I've been here for a while. Rachel told me I should wait in your office."

Luckily, her face was buried against his chest so he couldn't see her frown. *Rachel, you traitor!* "You should have come back into the workshop and said something."

"I didn't want to disturb you."

Like the feel of his fingers at the small of her back wasn't disturbing? Julia allowed herself a few seconds of comfort in his embrace. Reluctantly, she wiggled out of his hold, pretending to fiddle with her hair.

It was a nervous habit she thought she'd broken after high school. But no, here she was, twisting her hair around her finger like some coy fool. Almost instantly, she dropped her hands to her sides.

"You look tired," he said. "Beautiful, but exhausted."

"I'm fine, I'm good."

"I suspected that about you," he replied, an easy smile on his lips.

She backed up until she encountered the wall. "I've been thinking."

His face contorted in a playfully exaggerated grimace. "Guys learn early on that nothing good ever follows 'I've been thinking.' It's right up there with 'It isn't you, it's me.'"

She smiled in spite of herself. "Guilty. But seriously, Luke. Staying on your boat is, well, it probably isn't a good idea. We're pretty volatile together."

His grin broadened as he looked at her with those dark, smoldering eyes. "Just so I know, is your hesitation because you don't want anything to happen between us, or because you know it probably will?"

"The latter. The former—both." She blew out a breath of frustration, emotional and sexual. Tilting her head back, she met his gaze. "What happened to 'We'll take this slow,' and all that other stuff you said?"

He lifted his broad shoulders in a half-hearted shrug, as if the answer was obvious. "I kissed you."

"And?"

He reached her in two strides, then rested his hands at her waist. She breathed in the scent of his cologne and felt the ever-present stirring in her belly intensify. "Six years ago was fate. Think about it," he insisted. "Vegas is a big place. What were the odds that we'd keep running into each other?"

Pretty good, since the DEA arranged all those "accidental" encounters.

"First, I got that coupon for dinner at the restaurant where you worked. Then the gift shop was out of aspirin, so I had to go to the corner drugstore and there you were, buying a bottle of water. You could have bought water anywhere, but you were there.

"When I went to register for the convention, there you were again, handing out samples to earn extra money. See?" he said, taking her firmly by the shoulders. "We were meant to be together. I took one look at those incredible eyes of yours and—" He stopped, sucking in a deep breath as he cupped her cheek. "Well, I just *knew,* Julia. I know that sounds corny, but it's the truth."

One hand came to rest at the side of her neck, his fingers gently kneading the tight muscles. His warm breath spilled over her upturned face when he spoke.

"Knew what?" she asked, feeling her whole body go rigid. *Why did I ask the question? Do I want to hear the answer?*

"That I love you," he said softly, murmuring the words against her forehead, punctuating them with feathery kisses.

Her palms flattened against his chest, right above the even, rhythmic beat of his heart. "Lust is more like it," she suggested, more to convince herself than him. "Normal people don't fall in love on such short notice."

"Why not?"

"Because…well, because it takes time and familiarity. You can't love someone you don't know."

"Who says?"

"Reality. Logic. Reasoning—all the things that got us higher up on the food chain."

She felt his heart speed up beneath her

palm as he said, "You want reality? Well, I've never felt this way about another woman. Not even close. Logically, it seems like a waste of time to spend months and years sharing dinners and movies just to reinforce what I already know. So, by my reasoning, we should cut to the chase. Lay it all out there. No pretenses, no games. Life, I've discovered, is a lot simpler when you're completely open and honest about things. Don't you agree?"

Her head was spinning. Until this assignment was completed, she couldn't be honest with him. And a relationship couldn't build and grow on a foundation of lies and half-truths.

She couldn't be open. Miami Confidential insisted, quite correctly in Julia's opinion, on their agents maintaining top secrecy during a case. The fewer people who knew what and who was involved, the tighter the case they could build.

All intel was on a need-to-know basis. It was safer for all of them that way.

So it didn't matter what she wanted right now. She had to consider all the other players. Which meant that none of this was simple.

She looked into Luke's eyes and thought what she couldn't say aloud. *I love you, too*.

His expression grew more serious. "I'm looking for a response here. Anything. A nod, a—"

"Let's go back to the boat," she said with urgency. Since she couldn't *tell* him how she felt, she'd show him. Would it be enough?

During the brief ride to the marina next door, Julia discreetly punched in the code to Jeff's pager, sending the signal that he was no longer needed.

Luke parked, cut the engine, and they practically bolted toward the boat. Julia was almost overcome by the powerful rush surging to every nerve in her body. It was time, finally. The sensation was fueled by the fact that Luke kissed her hungrily as he steered her down the dock.

He helped her aboard, then lifted her in his arms and carried her to his cabin.

Gently, he set her down at the foot of the bed. She looked into his eyes and saw tangible proof that everything he'd said was true. Never, *ever*, had anyone looked at her with such open adoration. It touched something deep inside her, speaking directly to her most secret longings.

Luke's face was masked in raw emotion. Reaching up, she ran her finger along the strong, chiseled line of his jaw. Forget the rules. She couldn't do this. Not yet. Not without telling him the truth. "There's something I think you should know."

He placed his finger against her lips as he pulled her into the cradle of his thighs. Any doubts she might have had regarding his desire were instantly dispelled. He gathered her hair up in his hands and kissed her throat until Julia actually shivered. "Really, Luke," she pleaded, drawing an unsteady breath. "I have to tell you—"

"There's no hurry. I don't need the words, Julia. Not yet, anyway," he murmured as his hand came up to test the weight of her breast through the fabric of her shirt.

"But—"

He pulled her hard against him. "I've wanted to touch you like this for six years," he whispered. "Don't make me wait another second."

Her world spun as his hands swept through her hair, down her back, to her hips. His fingers danced against her skin, caressing her softly as he lowered his mouth to hers.

She should have settled things first; she knew it was the right thing to do. As his thumb brushed her erect nipple, suddenly right and wrong didn't matter. The only thing that did was the feel of his hands moving on her body. Stark and intense, her longing kicked in, six years of banked desire making her frantic. What if something happened to separate them again? Julia knew she couldn't take it. If nothing else, she would have this night to remember, and she wanted it. Desperately.

Her fingers fought with the buttons of his shirt. She needed to feel him, all of him.

"We'd better slow down, honey," he laughed as he took her wrists, spun her gently, then guided her downward so that she was beneath him on the mattress. "We've got all night."

Yes, she thought, *at least this one night.* Urgency and desire surged through her body, filling her with impatience as she tugged at his shirt. "Take this off."

He chuckled at the demand behind her breathy request. "Ladies first." In a few deft moves he stripped off her clothing. A low, appreciative rumble sounded in his throat when he dipped his head to take her nipple into his mouth.

She gasped with pleasure, her hands falling away from his shirt. Instead, she grabbed fistfuls of the bedspread as wave after wave of new sensations exploded through her. When his teeth nipped at her, Julia thought she might die then and there.

Not exactly a virgin, she'd never been a player, either. The few men in her life had never measured up after she'd given her heart to Luke.

Her hands roamed his skin, pulling him closer. She wanted something, everything, but she didn't know how to ask. "Luke, I…"

His head came up and his chocolate eyes roamed over her body. Her skin was damp and small shudders claimed her as his big hands stroked her feverish flesh.

"Tell me what you want," he murmured.

Her only response was a primal moan. He understood the frantic way her small hands touched and tugged at him; he felt the same. He wanted to go slow, to make up for the time they'd lost, but he smelled her shampoo, tasted the heated smoothness of her skin. And her eyes, all smoky and heavy-lidded with passion, urged him on. She responded to his every touch, matching him move for move. No woman had ever made him feel so much a man.

He left her only long enough to shed his

clothes. As he returned to her, she reared up like a mythical mermaid from the sea of rumpled covers, all hair and eyes and breasts. Her skin was the color of rich caramel, with a faint, rosy flush. She invited him with her outstretched arms, welcomed him as he slid in next to her, then pressed her warm breasts against his chest as she nibbled his neck and shoulders.

She was temptation personified with her parted, full lips and her shallow breaths. Seeing her need, he kissed her with a controlled savagery that surprised even him.

"I need to be inside you."

"Yes," she agreed without hesitation against his open mouth. "You do."

He rolled again, pressing her down on the mattress. Her hands grasped his hips as she arched toward him, her eyes glowing with passion. "Hurry."

Using his body, he moved her thighs apart. He held her gaze. "Tell me what you want."

She licked her lower lip. "You."

He drove inside her in one motion, silently cursing his lack of finesse. Julia must have sensed something because she stilled. "What?"

Gritting his teeth, Luke felt beads of perspiration form on his brow as he struggled for some measure of control. He wanted this to be incredible for her. If she kept writhing beneath him, he'd last about as long as a teenager on prom night.

She boldly wrapped her legs around him, pulling him deeper. Her fingers bit into the flesh of his hips.

"Don't..." he begged in a husky voice.

Her tongue came out to flick his nipple, and Luke lost the fight for control, giving in to the overpowering, primitive desire between them. He took her urgently, building quickly to match her frenzied need.

He stretched her, filled her, kissed her. Her hands stroked over the sweat-slicked muscles of his back. Her fingers fluttered over the valley of his spine. Her palms cupped him, pulled him closer.

She strained against him, clinging to him. He felt her climax, then his consciousness dimmed as he exploded inside of her.

Drained, Luke collapsed to the side. It took maybe two minutes before he could find the energy to say, "That was amazing."

"Yes, it was," she readily agreed in a voice almost too faint to hear.

"But it was way too fast. Sorry."

She rolled against him, draping one

shapely leg across his thigh. Her fingertip traced the outline of his nipple as she bent her head, hiding her expressive face with a curtain of hair. "You have nothing to be sorry for. I think I was the one who, um, kind of hurried things along."

Resting his forearm over his eyes, he was amazed that he could already feel the stirring returning to his groin. The knowledge brought a purely male grin to his lips. "Then we'll have to try again. You know, just to get it right?"

She dragged her mouth over his heated skin. "Sounds like a plan."

Shifting his weight, he turned so that he could see her face. He brushed a few strands of her silky hair back, revealing a satisfied expression. Her skin was flushed and her smile downright sinful. "Yes, it does," he agreed, gently pulling her into his arms.

It was hard for him to remain calm when she started raking her nails through the hair on his chest. "Where would you like me to start?" he teased.

Julia flattened her hands against his chest, enjoying the strong beat of his heart beneath her palms. Her eyes roamed boldly over the vast expanse of his shoulders, drinking in the sight of his impressive upper body. She openly admired his powerful thighs and washboard abs. "Don't ask me. My self-control seems to have gone right out the window."

She looked up at him, enjoying the anticipation fluttering in her stomach. Protected in the circle of his arms, Julia closed her eyes and allowed her cheek to rest against his chest. It would be wonderful to forget everything. Just for a few more hours. To pretend she was the woman he loved instead of the woman who'd deceived him from the get-go. Forget everything but the magic of being with him.

His fingers danced along her spine, leaving a trail of electrifying sensations in their wake. Like a spring flower, passion blossomed deep within her, filling her quickly with a frenzied desire she had never before known. He ignited feelings so powerful and so intense that Julia fleetingly wondered if this was possible. Then he moved the tip of his finger across her taut nipple and for a split second she couldn't think at all. Except maybe to consider begging for more when he stopped.

LUKE MOVED HIS HAND in slow, sensual circles until it rested against her rib cage, just under the swell of her breast. He wanted—no, needed—to see her face. He wanted to witness the desire in her eyes. Catching her chin between his thumb and forefinger, he tilted her head up with the intention of searching her eyes. He never made it that far.

His gaze was riveted on her slightly parted lips, which glistened in a sexy shade of pale rose, full and erotic and the exact same color as her nipples. His eyes roamed over every exotic feature, and he could feel her pulse rate increasing as he did so.

Lowering his head, he tasted her. Her mouth was warm and pliant, and so was her body, which again pressed urgently against him. His hands roamed purposefully, memorizing every nuance and curve.

He felt his own body respond with an ache, then an almost overwhelming rush of desire. Her arms slid around his waist, pulling him closer. Luke marveled at the perfect way they fit together. It was as if Julia had been made for him. For this.

"Julia," he whispered against her mouth. He toyed with a lock of her hair, then slowly wound his hand through the silken mass and gave a gentle tug, forcing her head back even more. Looking down at her face, Luke knew there was no other sight on earth as beautiful and inviting as her smoky-gray eyes. Nothing as sensual as her long, dark, curly hair fanned out against the pillow.

He began showering her face and neck with light kisses, telling her he loved her without saying a word. His mouth searched for that sensitive spot at the base of her throat. A pleasurable moan spilled from his mouth when she began running her palms over the tight muscles of his stomach.

Capturing both of her hands in one of his, Luke gently held them above her head. The position arched her back, drawing his eyes down to her erect nipples.

"This isn't playing fair," she said in a sexy, teasing tone.

"Believe me, Julia, it's better for both of us if I don't let you keep touching me," he assured her with a smile and a kiss.

Julia responded by lifting her body to his. The rounded swell of one exposed breast brushed his arm. His fingers closed over its fullness.

"Please let me touch you!" Julia cried out.

"Not yet," he whispered, ignoring her futile struggle to free her hands as he dipped his head to kiss the raging pulse point at her throat. Her soft skin grew hot as he worked his mouth lower and lower. She gasped when his lips closed around her nipple, then called his name in a hoarse voice that caused a tremor to run the full length of his body.

Moments later, he lifted his head long enough to see her passion-laden expression and to tell her she was beautiful.

"So are you."

Whether it was the sound of her voice or the way she pressed herself against him, Luke neither knew nor cared. He found himself nearly undone by the level of desire communicated by the movements of her supple body.

He sought her lips again as he released his hold on her wrists, and his body moved to cover hers, his tongue thrusting deeply into the warm recesses of her mouth. His hand moved downward, skimming her flesh all the way to her thigh. Then, giving in to the urgent need pulsating through him, Luke positioned himself between her legs. Every muscle tensed as he looked at her face before directing his attention lower, to the point where they would join.

Julia lifted her hips, welcoming, inviting,

as her hands fell to his waist and tugged him toward her.

"You're amazing," he groaned against her lips.

"I want you, she whispered. "Now, please?"

He wasted no time responding to her request. In a single motion, he thrust deeply into her, knowing without question that he had found heaven on earth.

The sheer pleasure of being inside her sweet softness was very powerful. This time he kept the rhythm of their lovemaking at a slow, deliberate pace, enjoying each time he felt the small shivers of her body convulsing. Now that their hunger had been fed, he could leisurely treat her to a series of slow, building climaxes.

A long, pleasurable time later, Julia again wrapped her legs around his hips just as explosive waves surged from him. One after another, ripples of pleasure poured from him into her. Satisfaction had never been so sweet.

With his head buried next to hers, the sweet scent of her hair filled his nostrils. Luke reluctantly relinquished possession of her body. It took several minutes before his breathing slowed to a steady, satiated pace.

Rolling onto his side next to her, Luke

rested his head against his arm and glanced down at her. She was sheer perfection. He could have happily stayed next to her in the cramped aft bunk until the end of time.

"What were you about to tell me earlier?" he asked, certain that she would confess her true feelings. A woman couldn't make love like that unless her heart was involved.

Her lashes fluttered against her cheeks and he sensed a sudden change in the air. A definite chill stabbed him in the gut. She'd left him once before....

The chirp of her cell phone interrupted the heavy silence, and she jumped to answer as if it were a welcome lifeline. Distracted, he only half listened to her side of the conversation.

Luke closed his eyes. God, what a mess. He couldn't exactly judge her, could he? After all his lectures about truth, honesty and open communication, how was she going to feel when *she* discovered the truth?

Chapter Thirteen

"What do you mean, you have to go?" Luke thundered, his voice reverberating through the cabin.

Julia was just about dressed when his hand snaked out and caught her wrist. His jaw was clenched and she read confusion and anger in his eyes.

"I have to go," she insisted, making a futile attempt to pull free from his hold. "It's work related," she hedged. "Jeff is on his way. He'll be here in a matter of minutes."

"Jeff," Luke repeated, dropping her wrist so he could pull on his jeans. In the process, he grabbed a small clock off the headboard. "He's the music director for Weddings Your Way, right? Are you actually trying to tell me there's a song selection emergency at...*four* in the morning?"

"I'm just telling you I have to go and it's

work related," Julia insisted, feeling a downward pull on her heart when she saw his expression darken. "I'll explain it all to you later. Right now, I have to leave."

"Like hell," Luke growled, gently taking her by the shoulders. "You're not going anywhere until you start making sense."

"There's been a development in Sonya's kidnapping."

"They found her?"

"No," Julia answered. "But there's a lead and I have to act on it."

Luke cocked his head to one side, confusion in his eyes. "Act on it? Doing what? Altering the suits for the detectives so they can investigate this lead?"

She brought her hands up in a smooth move and broke his hold, using her legs and the element of surprise to send him sprawling back onto the bed. She knew she hadn't hurt him, but it seemed the most expedient way to make the point. Plus, she hoped it would put him off balance enough so she could say what she had to say and make a fast exit. She doubted he'd want her around long once he knew the truth.

He lay there, stunned. "What the hell was that?"

"It's called subduing the aggressor," Julia explained. "See, I can do a lot more than sew. I'm well trained."

"In what? By whom?"

Julia hopped from one foot to the next as she slipped on her sandals. "Originally by the DEA."

He looked up at her blankly. "You aren't making any sense."

"Well," she muttered between tightly clenched teeth, focusing on the job at hand instead of her breaking heart. "I hadn't planned on explaining this in sixty seconds or less. But here goes. I was undercover for the DEA when we met in Vegas. My assignment was to get close to you in order to set up the sting that took down Esterhaus."

He blinked, propping himself up on his elbows. "You're joking, right?"

She wished, but if anything, the joke was on her. "No, Luke. The whole thing was orchestrated from the start. The DEA arranged all those accidental meetings between us. I needed you to get to Esterhaus."

He sat up. "So, what, you're still undercover?" She could see from the look in his eyes that he was quickly processing the information. "Who's your target this time?

A.J.?" Barely controlled anger turned the question into an accusation.

"No," she answered as she glanced out the small porthole and saw the headlights of Jeff's car as he pulled into the parking lot. "I mean, yes, I'm still undercover, but not for the DEA. It's complicated, Luke." She should have been honest before making love with him, but she didn't regret their passion. And maybe he would be willing to listen once she returned. "I really have to go. Jeff will cover you until I get back."

He rose to his feet, and although he didn't come closer, Julia felt stalked. "Cover me, why? And back from where? What the hell is going on?"

She closed her eyes, then looked up at the ceiling before turning back to him. "I work for a private company. I could—and probably will—lose my job for telling you this, but we do what traditional law enforcement can't. We've got two things going on right now. Getting Sonya Botero back safely, and protecting you."

"I don't need protecting," he shouted, his anger no longer controlled or concealed. He raked his hands through his hair.

"Yes, you do," she said. "I found the letters

in your drawer and I heard the threatening message on your machine."

Betrayal was written clearly on his face. "When?"

"I found them when I was getting your clothes," she explained, reluctantly moving toward the door.

"You've been playing me?" he asked. "In Vegas and again now?"

"Not totally," she insisted, wishing she had more time. She paused in the doorway. "Tonight, us, together. That had nothing to do with my job."

His response was an angry glare.

She felt pulled apart. Especially when she saw the hurt and fury shimmering in his dark eyes. Needing to make it better, or at least try, she said, "I love you, Luke, but I *really* have to go. We can talk when I get back."

"Pass, thanks," he said, his tone an angry sneer. "You don't love me, Julia. You can't— you don't even exist. You've just been playing a part all this time. Well, it's over. I wouldn't believe anything that came out of your mouth right now even if your tongue came notarized. You know the way out, and do me a favor?"

"Anything," she breathed sincerely, her heart hanging by a thread of hope.

"Don't bother coming back."

"Luke?" His name came out sounding like a pained plea. Which it was.

"Go," he practically barked. "Now."

"TOOK IT BADLY, did he?" Rafe asked thirty minutes later as they sped down A1A.

Dr. Ramon Morales was holed up in a condo in southwest Miami. The sole reason her boss had put her back on the Botero case was because Rachel suspected that Morales was the one responsible for nearly killing Sonya's driver, Craig Johnson. Though Juan had pulled some strings and gotten a photograph from the Laderan authorities, Julia was the only one who'd glimpsed Johnson's attacker at the hospital. She would know on sight if Morales was the right height and build.

She twisted her hair and fastened it with a clip, then checked her weapon before concealing it in the holster strapped to her calf. "About as well as Rachel will take it when I tell her I broke the pledge."

Rafe shrugged. "She'll be miffed, but she'll get over it. Especially if you tell her you're in love with the guy."

Julia's chest seized when she remembered

the look in Luke's eyes when he'd told her to leave. "Why are men such jerks?" Only it wasn't just him. She hadn't been honest from the start. It still hurt.

Rafe chuckled. "Training," he teased. "Look, Jules, the guy will come around. He loves you."

"He loves 'absolutes' more," she acknowledged with a heavy sigh. "Let's just forget it for now. What's the plan?"

"According to the building manager, Dr. Morales goes to a coffee shop every morning at six. He walks, so I'm thinking once you make the ID, you can distract him, I grab him, we team up and take him back to the shop."

"*You* could distract him and *I* could grab him," Julia countered.

"We'll flip a coin," Rafe suggested.

The first rays of golden sunlight peeked over the horizon just as Rafe parked the SUV on the street across from the apartment building. Julia would have given her left arm for a cup of coffee. She'd gone without any meaningful sleep for so long, her body had actually gathered a second wind. But her brain wanted caffeine. And action. Sitting in the car gave her too much time to think about the hole she'd dug for herself with Luke.

She should have told him the truth before they had sex. *Which truth?* her guilty conscious asked. The truth about her job, or the truth about her feelings? The two were inextricably linked.

"Target acquired," Rafe said.

A true professional, Julia brought her full attention to the task at hand. One look at the man and she knew instantly that Morales and the man fleeing the hospital were one and the same. "Positive ID," she confirmed.

Since she'd lost the coin toss, Julia got out of the car, hurrying so that she was walking parallel to Morales. Rafe drove past her, turning left at the first stop sign.

Julia waited until Morales was closer to the corner, then dashed across the street, frantically calling out to him. For effect, she first asked if he spoke Spanish, then added, "Can you help me, please?" with feigned panic in her voice.

Morales adjusted his tie, eyeing her suspiciously for a second before his shoulders relaxed. He sized her up, his black eyes lingering just a little too long on her breasts. "What is it you need?"

"I am looking for the Casa de la Relajación," she said. "I am late for an interview. I really need the job. I have two small children to care for. My mother is not well and I need to send money to—"

"I'm going in that direction," Morales said, placing his small, stubby fingers at her back. "Come, I will walk you there."

Julia let loose with effusive appreciation, purposefully babbling on so that Morales wouldn't notice the SUV idling at the curb. She was in the middle of telling Morales all about her fake daughter's fake troubles adjusting to kindergarten as they passed by the SUV.

Julia and Morales were even with the back bumper when Rafe appeared and discreetly shoved a gun into the target's back. Pretending to scratch her leg, Julia came up, training her weapon in the direction of Morales's gut just in case he had any thoughts of making a run for it.

"I have a little money and a watch."

"I don't think you'll be needing them for a while," Julia said. "Get in the car."

Rafe got behind the wheel while Julia slipped in beside Morales in the back seat. The childproof locks being activated sounded like gunshots. Sonya's image flashed in Julia's brain. She glared at Morales, nearly overwhelmed by the desire to shoot him in the leg just to cause him some pain.

"Where is she?" she asked, body angled toward him, the Sig comfortable in her hands. If he so much as made a wrong move, she'd be delighted to shoot him somewhere vital and painful.

"I don't know what you're talking about," Morales replied, his tone even, his gaze unflinching. "I believe," he added, switching to perfect, unaccented English, "in this country I am entitled to an attorney if I don't wish to answer questions."

"Wrong," Rafe said. "We aren't law enforcement, Morales. You don't have any constitutional protection with us."

Julia saw a brief flicker of fear in the man's eyes. "Start talking," she prodded, nudging him in the rib cage with her gun. "Sonya Botero? Where is she?"

Rafe's phone rang. The call was quick, then he said, "The computer is finished enhancing the security tapes from the hospital. We got you, Morales. We can prove you tried to kill Craig Johnson. If you don't tell us where we can find Sonya and who orchestrated the kidnapping, we'll turn you over to the police. They'll give you a lawyer, then they'll convict you and put you in prison for the next twenty-five years."

A thin line of perspiration formed on Morales's upper lip. Julia let him mull over that possibility for a few seconds. "We have a better offer," she told him coldly.

"I'm listening," Morales said, covering his mouth as he let out a nervous cough.

"Is she alive?"

Morales nodded. "She was fine the last time I saw her. Unlike you, she is of no use dead."

Julia felt a wave of relief wash over her. *Thank God.*

Wait! her brain yelled. "Unlike me? You shot at me and blew up my apartment?"

Morales smiled a purely evil grin. "Had you walked a bit faster, you would have been blown to bits. As for the shooting incident, that wasn't my doing."

"If you're trying to curry favor," Julia warned, "you're going about it all wrong." She jabbed him again. Why would he admit to the bombing but not the shooting? It didn't gel.

"You almost killed Lu— us, *twice.*" Her anger intensified when she thought of how close this man had come to killing Luke. Now he was lying about it. *Bastard.*

"Just out of curiosity, why go after Julia?" Rafe asked from the front seat. "Is it because of her connection to the Botero family? Kidnap his daughter, and kill the woman he thinks of as a daughter? What did Botero do to you? What made you go from being a doctor to a kidnapper and a killer?"

Morales didn't answer.

One of Rafe's strengths was his focused ability to pepper a suspect with questions. The man could be unrelenting. Julia had no sympathy for Morales. They'd get answers from him, one way or another. She was silently fuming at the casual way he'd admitted to nearly killing her and Luke. She almost hoped the man dragged his feet. Then they'd have a reason to inflict a little well-deserved pain.

"Tell us what we want to know and we'll arrange for you to be flown back to Ladera as soon as Sonya is safely returned," Julia said.

Morales opened his mouth. Instead of words, foam bubbled from his lips and his eyes rolled back in his head.

"Son of a—" Julia tossed her gun in the

front seat, then straddled Morales, yanking on his tie. It was a wasted effort; the guy was already convulsing.

"Smell that?" Rafe asked, clearly pissed.

"Bitter almond," Julia groaned. "The SOB must have taken cyanide when he pretended to cough."

Morales went rigid, then died.

Julia didn't care that the man was dead, only that he hadn't given them any information. She wished there was some way to revive him, but she knew better. Grabbing his hands, she turned them over, spotting two more small tablets tucked between the links of his watchband.

She moved off Morales, shoving him out of sheer vexation. "Our only lead, and the little weasel suicides on us."

Rafe slowed the car as they approached the driveway to Weddings Your Way.

Being in the back seat of a car with a dead guy was not nearly as bad as seeing Carmen waiting on the doorstep.

"DUDE, YOU LOOK LIKE hell," A.J. remarked when Luke arrived at the job site trailer a few minutes before 7:00 a.m.

"I've already gotten that lecture from

Carmen," he growled. Normally, he would have been overjoyed to see A.J. holding up his end of the deal. He was there on time and showed no obvious signs of being high or hungover.

Only this morning, Luke was distracted thinking about Julia. He couldn't sleep, not when her perfume still clung to his pillow. Not when the memory of having her in his arms was so fresh. Not while knowing it had all been a lie.

He hadn't felt this betrayed in years. Understanding that her affections weren't real reminded him of his foster-home days. When the families only pretended to care if the social worker was visiting. As with Julia, he'd been nothing but a means to an end.

The foster families got their monthly stipend checks.

Julia got Esterhaus.

"So, what's my first assignment?" A.J. asked, following him into the trailer.

"Demo," Luke said, going to the drafting table. He rubbed his eyes, straining to focus on the blueprints. "See this?" He tapped one section of the page. "You're going to gut the inside of the yacht club."

"Way cool."

Luke sighed, then flipped on the coffee-maker. "Hard hat and safety glasses at all times." He paused, looking at A.J.'s flip-flops. "There's an extra pair of boots in the back of my truck."

"'Kay. Thanks. So, did you have a big fight with your girlfriend, or what?"

"Did you and Carmen compare notes?"

A.J. grinned. "Of course. You had to know she'd call me the minute she got off the phone with you."

Luke let out a small laugh. "Yeah, I suppose I did know."

"She's seriously mad at your girlfriend. Carmen told me she was even thinking about going to that fancy wedding shop to give that woman a piece of her mind."

Luke groaned inwardly. "Let's hope she has better things to do today. You do," he said, tossing A.J. a hard hat. "Tell the fore-man I'll be out in a minute. I'm just going to have a quick cup of coffee."

As the pot finished sputtering, the phone rang. He recognized the woman's voice im-mediately.

"NOW IS NOT THE BEST TIME," Julia said as she ushered Carmen Lopez into her office.

"Not for Luke, either," Carmen said as she sat down. Her normally placid, dark eyes practically spewed venom as they narrowed in Julia's direction. "I know him better than anyone," Carmen insisted in clipped, sharp syllables. "I know that six years ago, he was devastated when you left him. I heard that same devastation in his voice when I spoke to him this morning."

Julia glanced up at the clock. Didn't these people sleep? It was only a few minutes after seven and already they'd had time to compare notes and gossip?

"It wasn't intentional," Julia murmured with a calm she was far from feeling.

"I had no idea you were *that* Julia. Under the circumstances, I think we should go see your boss. I can't, in good conscience, allow you to continue working on my wedding. I don't want you anywhere near my brother."

Well, wasn't this day off to a smashing start? Luke hated her. Her only suspect in Sonya's kidnapping was dead. Rachel was about to learn that she'd told the closely guarded truth about Miami Confidential to an outsider. And now she was jeopardizing the Lopez-Mitchell wedding. What else could possibly go wrong?

The intercom buzzed. "Yes?"

"My office as soon as possible," Rachel said.

"I'm sorry, Carmen, but I really do have—"

"You're not getting off that easy," Carmen insisted.

What had happened to the soft-spoken, polite woman she'd been working with the last six months? This Carmen seemed more like a mother bear protecting a defenseless cub.

"I've been polite," Julia began, an instant headache slamming between her eyes. "But in all honesty, my relationship with Luke really isn't any of your business."

"It is now," she argued. "The man loves you."

"That isn't always enough."

"Of course it is," Carmen said. "You've probably had unconditional love your whole life. For people like Luke and me, it's a precious commodity. Not something to be tossed aside or ignored. I don't understand how you could do this to him. You are the most uncaring, cruel, heartless—"

Julia made the letter T with her hands. *Time out, lady!* "He tossed me out on my rear," she snapped. "And FYI, I am in love with him."

Carmen blinked her pretty dark eyes. "Then what's the problem?"

The intercom buzzed a second time. Rachel impatiently commented that she was still waiting. "I really can't do this right now," Julia told Carmen. "You can wait, but I don't know how long I'll be."

Carmen settled back in the chair. "I'll be right here, thank you."

Julia stepped out of the proverbial frying pan and headed down the hallway into the fire.

Rachel was seated behind her desk. The minute Julia walked into the room, those clear blue eyes fixed on her. Rachel straightened a stack of papers on her desk.

"Sit down."

I am so fired. "I take it you know I, um, told Luke the truth."

"Yes. We tapped his phone, and from the gist of conversation he had with Carmen this morning, I assumed as much."

"I can explain," Julia began, but snapped her mouth closed when Rachel gave a little shake of her head.

"We can deal with that later."

"Is this about Morales dying on my watch? Because I have to tell y—"

Again Rachel shook her head, cutting her off with a quick dismissive hand gesture. "Rafe's already disposing of that problem. Though I'm sorry he killed himself before the two of you could get anything out of him."

Me, too.

"The notes you found at Luke's place had only two sets of prints. Yours and Luke's."

Julia sighed. "Dead end."

"Yes, but the medical records were more telling." Rachel passed them across the desk. "Betty Anderson's broken arms? They were radial fractures."

"Someone twisted her arm until it broke?" Julia asked.

"Yes, and that someone did it long after her husband was killed."

Her brain ignored the lurch of nausea in her stomach. "Unless she hooked up with another loser, it had to be A.J. or Tommy. I think we can safely eliminate Carmen as a potential suspect. Though she's in my office right now and she's pretty pissed."

"I told you I thought there was something hinky about that family. So I did a little more digging."

"Yes?" Her headache thumped in time with her heartbeat.

"Two things. First, Betty Anderson's credit card statements show she ordered a semi-automatic and a conversion kit two months ago from a dealer in North Carolina."

"Morales said he didn't shoot at me. If it was Betty Anderson, she had to be aiming for Luke."

"Except I've already confirmed that Betty was delivering meals to shut-ins at the time of the shooting."

Julia's mind raced as she fit the puzzle pieces into place. "It has to be Tommy. He could easily get access to his mother's credit cards and mailing address. He'd have to use her because with his arrest record, he'd never be able to buy a gun legally."

"Or she's helping him," Rachel offered. "Either voluntarily or because he hurts her."

"Why now?" Julia wondered aloud. "If it's revenge because Luke killed Frank Anderson, why wait almost twenty years?"

"I don't know, but I suggest you start by asking Carmen."

"I'll go straight to Luke," she said as she shot out of the chair.

"Start with Carmen," Rachel repeated.

"Why? Right now she'd like to bite my head off. I don't think she'll be in any great hurry to open up to me."

"Because of this," Rachel said, sliding another document to Julia.

Julia read the paper twice. It was a twenty-year-old doctor's report from an ER in Broward County dated the day after Frank Anderson's murder. Thirteen-year-old Carmen Lopez had been brought in hemorrhaging. According to the intake notes, her boyfriend had informed the staff that Carmen was suffering a miscarriage.

Julia felt physically ill. "Luke and Carmen were…"

"Carmen is about to marry into a very wealthy family. I doubt she wants them to know she was sleeping with her foster brother."

She lifted her eyes off the report. "You think Carmen tried to kill Luke?"

"It would explain the time discrepancy. That she had a thing going with her foster brother who happens to be a convicted murderer might be a secret she'd kill to protect."

"Not if I kill her first," Julia muttered as she returned to her office. It was empty.

She raced down the stairs and found Vicki seated at her desk. "Thank God you're here early. Did you see Carmen Lopez?"

Vicki nodded. "I put a call through to her in your office. She took it, then bolted out of here."

"Who called?"

"Luke Young."

Chapter Fourteen

"Stop him!" Julia yelled into the cell phone. "Don't let Luke leave with Carmen. I'll be there in less than two minutes."

"Okay," Jeff said. "I'll wait for you."

Julia jumped into her Jeep, gunned the engine and started to pull out of the driveway. A moving van blocked her, so she lay on her horn.

"Come on, come on," she groaned as the truck lumbered up the street for what felt like an hour.

There wasn't enough room for her to pass the truck, so the two-minute trip ended up taking closer to five. Julia tore down the road to the marina, relieved when she saw Jeff's car still in the lot.

Barely stopping long enough to put the gearshift in Park, she leaped from the Jeep and dashed down the dock.

"Luke?" she called, moving below deck as she called his name twice more.

She grabbed the cell phone from her belt clip and pressed redial. Jeff didn't answer. A sense of dread spurred her on.

She left the boat and raced to Jeff's car. It, too, was empty. Glancing around, she spotted the construction trailer and ran to it. She heard the pounding of hammers from the building being rehabbed. It echoed the pounding of her heart.

Her hand was on the knob when she heard a muffled groan. Jerking open the door, she found Jeff on all fours.

"What happened?" she asked, grasping his arm to help him up. "Where's Luke?"

He held his jaw as he got to his feet. "I'm fine, thanks," he muttered under his breath. "Your boyfriend cold-cocked me."

"Why?"

"How the hell should I know?" Jeff answered. "First the kid comes running back here—"

"What kid?"

"The druggie, A.J. Then a few minutes later, Carmen shows up. You called. I walked in here and told Luke you wanted him to stay put, and the next thing I know I'm seeing stars."

Julia pressed her fingers to her temples as she ran all the possibilities in her mind. "Come on," she said, grabbing the sleeve of Jeff's shirt and practically dragging him out of the trailer.

"Where are we going?"

"I'll know in a minute," she said, dialing her phone. When Vicki answered, Julia asked, "I need you to check the phone tap and let me know if anyone called Luke's job site." Vicki provided the answer in a matter of seconds. Then Julia asked for Betty Anderson's address.

"West Broward," she told Jeff. "Get in."

"Want to fill me in?"

What she wanted was the ability to fly. Traffic was horrible on I-95 this time of the morning. As she weaved illegally in and out of the commuter traffic, much to the annoyance of the other drivers, she told Jeff what she knew.

"That sweet, demure woman is the one who peppered the office with bullets?" he asked, looping his hand through the leather strap as they skidded along the shoulder.

"Looks that way," Julia said. "Betty Anderson called Luke this morning. She said she was hurt and needed his help."

"So Betty and Carmen are in this together?"

Julia shook her head and let out a long, pensive breath. "Maybe. We're missing something. If Carmen's goal is to get rid of anyone who knew her secret, then why involve Betty Anderson as an accomplice?"

"Unless Betty already knows," Jeff suggested. "If Carmen was just a kid, chances are she confided her, er, *situation* to her mother."

"You're right. Unless there was a reason she couldn't."

Julia winced. "Wrong guy," she said, slapping her palms against the steering wheel. "Luke wasn't the father of Carmen's baby."

"A.J. and Tommy would have been too young."

"That leaves the late Frank Anderson," Julia agreed. The reason why Luke had murdered his foster father was starting to form an ugly picture.

"Which makes Betty a better suspect than Carmen. Her gun, her murdered husband."

"But twenty years is a long time to plot revenge," Julia repeated. "Why would she wait two decades? Let's back up. If she wanted Luke to be punished for killing her husband, why did she go to the judge on his behalf?"

They would know soon enough, she

thought as she cut across four lanes of traffic to exit the highway. What if she was wrong?

She tossed Jeff her phone. "Call Rachel and fill her in. See if some of the other agents can go by A.J.'s apartment just in case." Seeing the obstacle up ahead, she did a quick mental calculation, then added, "Hold tight." Lights flashed a warning, but she swerved around the lowered railway-crossing barricades, completely ignoring the oncoming train. The Jeep bounced over the tracks.

Julia missed the street, slammed on the brakes, backed up and fixed the error. The smell of burning rubber wafted up from the undercarriage of the vehicle. She couldn't have cared less.

The sparsely populated area was home to orange groves and the occasional house. They drove about two miles down the road when she spotted Luke's SUV parked in one of the driveways. Relief surged through her. The Anderson place. A neat little yellow house with neglected window boxes devoid of plants.

"See anything?" she asked as she pulled off on the shoulder, and only then remembered that she'd left her gun in the SUV with Rafe. She'd have to improvise.

Jeff pulled his weapon from his ankle

holster and got out of the Jeep. She'd parked at the point in the road where the street blended into a dirt drive. Julia climbed out in turn and was getting ready to join him when a shot rang out.

She dived to one side of the drive, rolling on the hard ground. Jeff did the same, in the opposite direction.

"I'll go right," he said. "Can you make it to that side door?"

Julia nodded just as two more shots rang out from inside the house. Ignoring all the safeguards she'd been taught about teamwork, she abandoned Jeff and made a beeline for the front door. She was vaguely aware that Jeff was cursing a blue streak, but she was more fixated on getting inside. To Luke.

She reached for the doorknob but yanked her hand away when another bullet splintered the wood from the inside. Who was shooting and why?

"Put the gun down, Tommy."

She recognized Luke's voice and her heart swelled with unbridled joy.

"Go to hell."

"Please, Tommy, don't do this," Carmen whimpered. "We can help you."

"You owe me," Tommy retorted.

Julia peered through a small crack between the blind and the door. She had a partial view of Luke. He was backed into a corner, with Carmen tucked behind him.

Where was A.J.?

Julia's jaw clenched as she contemplated her next move. Sunlight glinted off the barrel of Tommy's gun as he raised it in Luke's direction.

Julia reacted on instinct. She reared back and kicked in the door.

Tommy's finger twitched.

"Don't," she warned, really missing her gun.

Tommy's pale eyes jerked between Julia and where Luke shielded Carmen from harm.

"This is an unexpected complication," Tommy acknowledged in a flat monotone.

"Get out of here, Julia," Luke said.

"Too late." Tommy said, waving the gun between targets as an evil smile lifted the corners of his mouth. "Julia, is it?" he asked. "Did you know Luke prides himself on being the great protector? So, since you're here, let's play a little game of Who Will Luke Choose? just to make this interesting."

Carmen made a strangled noise.

Tommy jerked the gun toward Julia, then toward Carmen. "Which one, Luke? One of them will die before you can get to me. Carmen?" He swung the gun again. "Or Julia?" The gun jerked back. "Julia or Carmen?"

Julia didn't so much as flinch. "If I'm going to die, Tommy, I'd like to know why."

"They killed my father," he explained.

"Carmen had nothing to do with it," Luke insisted. "It was an accident."

Tommy's eyes flashed with hatred. "Six months ago I found a letter my mother wrote. I know Carmen seduced my father."

When Tommy's finger twitched on the trigger, Julia quickly intervened. "I heard it a different way."

It worked. Tommy's attention and his anger turned on her. "Shut up."

"Your father was a pedophile," Julia taunted.

"Julia, please don't," Luke muttered through clenched teeth. "This isn't helping."

"You didn't know my father," Tommy growled. "He took in all these losers and instead of gratitude, they killed him."

"So what? You're going to kill them and go to prison?"

Tommy shook his head. "No, I'm going to

kill you. A better plan than the original. I was going to pick you off one by one. That's why I shot up Weddings Your Way. But this is better. I'll kill you all and A.J. is going to prison."

"Where is A.J.?" Julia asked.

"In his old room staring at the ceiling, high as a kite. All I had to do was show him the needle, and his lack of willpower did the rest. He's the perfect patsy. Poetic justice, don't you think?"

"No, not really," Julia answered.

Tommy seemed surprised. "Luke, you bad boy. You didn't tell her the truth?"

"Shut up, Tommy."

"How very gallant," Tommy breathed, still waving the gun. "Well, Julia, I'll let you in on a little secret. Luke didn't—"

A single shot shattered the window before it tunneled into Tommy's temple. Julia breathed a huge sigh of relief.

"It took you long enough," she called out the door. "What were you waiting for, Jeff? A flaming invitation?"

"At least I brought my weapon," he countered when he entered the house.

Carmen's shoulders shook as she sobbed heavily in Luke's arms. He was patting her back, comforting her, but his eyes were fixed on Julia.

"Thank you," he said, as if he'd choke on the words.

Unable to stand the sting of his rejections a second time, Julia went to check on A.J.

As promised, he was in one of the bedrooms, a needle still stuck in his vein. Julia raked her hair back from her face, went over and used the hem of her shirt to pull the syringe out. "I think you need some detox."

"Sweet," he said, his words slurred. "You're Luke's girl."

"No, I'm not."

She helped A.J. into a sitting position so she could check his pulse. He would live until the ambulance showed up. She found Mrs. Anderson in a broom closet, gagged and beaten. Julia held her hand until help arrived.

During that time, Luke and Jeff bartered a plan. Neither he nor Carmen would tell the cops about Miami Confidential if Julia and Jeff agreed not to make reference to Carmen's abuse.

Worked for everyone. Including the authorities, who took statements and stories before finally telling them everyone was free to leave.

Julia waited, hoping Luke might speak to her, but it didn't happen. He walked Carmen to his car. *Always the protector,* Julia thought as she watched him drive away. For the first time in years, she felt the warm trail of tears fall from her eyes as she whispered, "Goodbye."

"RACHEL WANTS TO SEE YOU."

Julia pressed the intercom button and thanked Vicki. She'd been expecting this. Tommy had been dead more than a week and Carmen had married Dalton an hour ago, just as planned.

It had been eight long days since she'd last seen Luke. Eight and counting, she reminded herself as she pushed out of her chair for what she suspected might be the last time.

Sonya was still missing. Rachel had barely spoken two words to Julia. Her lone assignment had been to visit with Carlos, who was now recuperating at his estate, just to make sure Sean Majors wasn't keeping them out of the loop.

And now it was time to get fired.

No man, no house, no job—she was a regular country and western song. If it wasn't so pathetic, she might have laughed.

Rachel ushered her in, her expression revealing nothing. "Sit down."

"Can we do this quickly?"

"Do what?"

"Fire me. That's why I'm here, right?"

"Why would you think that?"

"No new assignments, most of my work has been passed off to one of the other agents. I just assumed—"

"Wrong," Rachel said. "I've cut back on some of your work, yes. But only because I needed to reassign things I thought would last longer than you'll be around."

"So, I'm not fired, just being transferred?"

"You're not being fired and you're not being transferred, exactly."

"What else is there?"

"Promotion," Rachel said. "I recommended you to lead the new office opening up in Palm Beach."

Julia was stunned. "Wow. I wasn't expecting that."

"You earned it," Rachel insisted. "Of course, it will take some time to set up the new office. A few months, maybe."

"What's the cover?"

"A restaurant."

"This is amazing. Thank you."

"For right now, I have an assignment for you." Rachel slid a folded slip of paper across her desk. "I need you to go to this address in an hour. Your contact will meet you."

ARMED WITH ONLY an address, Julia sped north along the coastline. Delray Beach was about a forty-five minute drive from Miami. Like most of south Florida, the area ran the full gamut from multimillion-dollar estates to modest trailer parks and everything in between. She guessed Rachel was sending her to meet with the new client because of the location. Delray was right about halfway between Miami and Palm Beach.

Spotting the pink stucco columns on the east side of the road that Rachel had listed as her landmark, Julia slowed and turned right.

Her Jeep lumbered down the rutted, unpaved drive. Uneasiness affected the tiny hairs at the nape of her neck, causing them to stand on end.

A tiny For Sale sign hung askew in the yard, rusting from the salt air. The small house was in serious disrepair, though it was a killer location and no more than fifty yards from the beach.

"Hello?" she called.

There wasn't another car in sight. Maybe the new client was late.

Julia tried the front door. It dangled precariously from a single hinge before reluctantly scraping across the floor. "Anyone home?" She glanced around the dusty, deteriorating interior and smelled...bacon? "What is this?" she wondered, spying a blanket spread out on the floor, holding glasses and candles and a small picnic basket.

Luke.

He peeked around the corner and offered her a bright smile along with a bottle of champagne. "Hi."

"Hi," she replied as her whole body stiffened anxiously.

"I liberated some food from the reception."

He walked in wearing the tux she'd altered. She let out a little laugh.

"What?" he asked, his dark brows drawn together.

"You've got a whole James Bond thing going on. You're in a tux, you're carrying champagne. It's a little...weird." And a lot wonderful, seeing him again after so long. She'd missed him badly.

He poured two flutes and brought her one. Her fingers sizzled at the contact. Her pulse shot up and it felt like her heart might beat hard enough to break a few ribs.

"What's this about?" she asked.

He gazed down at her with those coffee-colored eyes and she felt her knees weaken. "I need to know if you still love me."

He was so close she could actually feel the heat from his body. She felt herself being drawn in as her brain started flashing a warning. Julia took one step back. "Wait a minute. Rachel sent me here. How did you pull that off?"

He flashed her a grin. "Some people find me charming."

When he reached for her, Julia ducked, but not before she saw an envelope tucked in the breast pocket of his jacket. She recognized the personalized stationary straightaway. "You have a note for me?"

He patted the pocket. "For later. Right now…" He switched his champagne to one hand and hooked the other around her waist.

Pressed against him, feeling his breath against her skin—it was all too much. Closing her eyes, she battled back tears.

"Your lip is quivering," Luke whispered

against her ear. "I didn't think secret agents cried."

Halfheartedly, she smacked his solid bicep. "I'm not a secret agent. I'm more of an investigator."

"Which is why I hired you for the day."

"To do what?"

"For what it cost me," he joked, "you should have to stand on your head and juggle while I talk. To investigate, of course." He led her over to the blanket and tugged gently at her wrist until she joined him.

"What am I investigating?"

"Me."

She eyed him suspiciously. "What kind of game is this?"

"The kind with shrimp wrapped in bacon, and canapés and champagne, and whatever else Carmen had them pack in this thing."

"How was the wedding?" Julia asked, adjusting the hem of her skirt just for something to do.

"Lavish. Fun."

"Good."

"A.J. wasn't there. He's back at the Keller Center. Doing well."

"Good."

"You could have come to the wedding."

"It seemed inappropriate under the circumstances."

He reached out and lifted her chin, forcing her to meet his gaze. "Julia, I made a huge mistake."

"No, you were right. I should have told you the truth sooner." *Maybe then...*

"I was reminded recently that there are times when keeping a secret is the only option."

"Reminded by whom?"

"Carmen," he said. "Do you remember that Tommy started to say something before Jeff shot him?"

She nodded.

"He was about to tell you that it was Carmen who killed Frank Anderson."

Julia blinked. "What?"

"He was beating Betty and, since you called him a pedophile, I'm guessing that you know what he'd been doing to Carmen, right?"

Julia nodded and brushed the hair off her face. "But you went to jail."

He shrugged. "I was the best choice. Carmen was too young and Betty was too fragile. We agreed that I'd be the one to take responsibility."

"What happened?"

"Betty caught Frank attacking Carmen. The two of them started fighting. When Frank started beating Betty, Carmen couldn't handle it. She was thirteen, abused, pregnant and full of rage. I guess she just snapped. She went out into the yard and grabbed a rock. She hit Frank. I don't think she really meant to kill him, she just wanted him to stop."

"Of course not," Julia agreed. "Why not just tell the truth? Those sound like pretty extenuating circumstances."

"Now, sure," he agreed easily. "Twenty years ago beating your wife was a family matter and jurors didn't think fathers—real, step or foster—would rape their daughters. Back then, we were afraid to take the chance. Carmen could have been tried as an adult and sent to prison for the rest of her life."

"So could you."

"I'm tough."

She reached up and cupped his cheek in her hand. Her heart swelled when he leaned into her touch. Setting aside the champagne glasses, Julia kissed him deeply.

Luke pulled back and quietly searched her face. "After what I said to you, this is the part where you get to call me a hypocrite. You can even slap me."

"Slap you?" she scoffed. "I'm a highly trained agent. I could kill you with a swizzle stick if I wanted to."

"Do you want to?" he asked.

He held his breath awaiting her answer. Julia decided not to hold him in suspense. "No. I think what you did for Carmen and Betty was stupid, but very sweet."

"Am I forgiven? And can we start over?"

"You may not want to. I'm getting a new job."

He looked surprised. "Where?"

"Palm Beach. But not for a few months."

Slowly, his mouth pulled into a broad grin.

"What?" she asked. "Why are you smiling like the Cheshire cat?"

He wrapped her in his arms and kissed her slowly until her head was swimming through a blissful fog. She looked up at him with open adoration. "At least tell me why you had Rachel arrange this meeting."

"Rachel. Right," he said, reaching into the pocket of his jacket. "She said if you forgave me for being an ass—her exact words—I was supposed to give you this."

Julia flicked her nail under the flap and

tore open the note. She smiled as she realized the wisdom behind the single line: NOW YOU HAVE BALANCE.

"Is that secret agent code?" he asked.

She laughed. "No. Rachel once told me that I'd be better at my job when I had balance in my life. Now I know what she meant."

"I don't."

"You," Julia said, brushing her lips against his. Hunger stirred in the pit of her stomach and it had nothing to do with the food nearby. "Having you in my life. It's balance. Before, all I had was my work. Now I have…more."

"Which is another aspect of this we have to address."

She squeezed her eyes closed. "No, no!" she joked. "Not the mandatory lining up of the ducks!"

"That is my thing," Luke reminded her as he playfully tugged a few strands of her hair. "What do you think of the house?"

Julia looked around while Luke fed her some grapes. "I like that you can hear the ocean," she said. "How many bedrooms?"

"Three," he said, taking her hands and pulling her to her feet. He tucked her into the cradle of his embrace as he led her around the home. "Right here, there'll be a state-of-the-art kitchen. All the bells and whistles like on the TV shows. And a dishwasher that doesn't sound like Sherman's army is approaching."

Julia felt a lump of emotion settle in her throat. He was repeating her words verbatim and she was genuinely touched.

"A modest pool out back, with a sundeck."

"Luke?" She choked out his name as tears filled her eyes. "You're going to build my house?"

"I've still got some papers to sign. I was waiting for your approval."

"It'll be great," she said enthusiastically. "You found a perfect location and there's a marina just down the street so you can dock there. You'll have—"

"Not *that* kind of approval," he said, bracketing her shoulders in his hands. "The kind where you say yes, Luke, I love you, I want to marry you and live in this house with you."

She frowned. "I have to decide all that right now?"

He stilled and she felt his fingers tighten. "Not if you don't want to."

Slowly, deliberately, she grinned up at

him, feeling him relax. "Could we screen in a small lanai? If you'll do that, then yes, I do love you and I'll marry you and—ouch!"

Her teasing earned her a swat on the bottom. "I'll build you a lanai if you'll show me how that whole swizzle stick thing works."

"I could do that, if you'll do something for me?"

He kissed her forehead. "Are we going to negotiate everything?"

"Probably."

"Okay," he sighed. "What do you want me to do for you?"

"Tell me you love me."

"I'll do you one better than that." He scooped her up in his arms. "Not only will I tell you how much I love you," he promised, kissing her between each word, "I'll show you."

* * * * *

Don't miss the next book in the suspenseful
MIAMI CONFIDENTIAL *series*
when Mallory Kane presents
COVERT MAKEOVER,
coming in July 2006
only from Harlequin Intrigue.

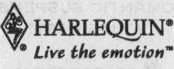

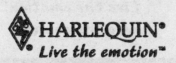

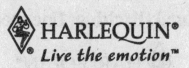

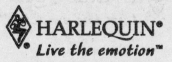

Harlequin Historicals®
Historical Romantic Adventure!

From rugged lawmen and valiant knights to defiant heiresses and spirited frontierswomen, Harlequin Historicals will capture your imagination with their dramatic scope, passion and adventure.

Harlequin Historicals . . . they're too good to miss!

❤ Silhouette

SPECIAL EDITION™

Emotional, compelling stories that capture the intensity of living, loving and creating a family in today's world.

Special Edition features bestselling authors such as Nora Roberts, Susan Mallery, Sherryl Woods, Christine Rimmer, Joan Elliott Pickart— and many more!

For a romantic, complex and emotional read, choose Silhouette Special Edition.

passionate powerful provocative love stories

**Silhouette Desire delivers
strong heroes, spirited heroines
and compelling love stories.**

Desire features your favorite authors,
including

Annette Broadrick,
Ann Major,
Anne McAllister
and Cait London.

**Passionate, powerful and provocative
romances *guaranteed!***

For superlative authors, sensual stories
and sexy heroes, choose Silhouette Desire.

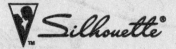

passionate powerful provocative love stories